2238

P9-CBT-067

2388

by
Carole Gift Page

Based on the Screenplay
by Edward T. McDougal

MOODY PRESS
CHICAGO

ISBN: 0-8024-5925-0

Moody Press, a ministry of the Moody Bible Institute, is designed for
education, evangelization, and edification. If we may assist you in knowing more about Christ and the Christian life, please write us without ob-
ligation: Moody Press, c/o MLM, Chicago, Illinois 60610.

1 2 3 4 5 6 7 Printing/VI/Year 91 90 89 88 87 86

Printed in the United States of America

1

After school today I took the elevated train down-town to the Chicago Loop where my dad, Sid Hughes, tapes his TV talk show. The weather was extra hot for May. I hated leaving the cool, clean suburbs for the sweltering city, but I was in a real bind. I needed my dad's help. In all my sixteen years he had hardly ever been there for me, so today I decided I would go to him.

I walked the two blocks to the television studios through wet, clinging humidity. The air was heavy with hot diesel fumes and the shrill screech of tires on burning pavement. The streets were already clogged with late afternoon traffic deserting the city for the su-burbs, and the sidewalks were crowded with shoppers.

At last I spotted the huge, glittering marquee an-nouncing THE SID HUGHES SHOW. Shifting my books under my arm, I slipped with my usual reluc-tance inside the wide double doors. I caught my breath as the sudden onrush of artificial cold slapped my face. The noise, confusion, and smells of the con-crete city were gone—shut out. I stood on thick, plush carpet, surrounded by velvet wallpaper and a vacuum of silence. I was in my father's world—a world of glamour, prestige, and power.

As I walked past the receptionist's desk toward Studio C, Mary, the receptionist, called cheerily, "Hello, Tim! How's school?"

"Great! No problem." Always the same question, always the same reply.

"Your dad's taping now."

"Yeah, I know. I'll wait."

I wasn't crazy about dropping in on my dad when he was in the middle of a taping, but I knew he wouldn't be home until late, and I needed advice fast. My grade in career planning was at stake. I had to write a paper on what I wanted to be—you know the old spiel—doctor, lawyer, Indian chief, that sort of thing. I didn't have the slightest idea what I wanted to be. That's why I figured I'd better check things out with my dad at the studios.

Let me say right up front that I never feel comfortable hanging around the television studio. Everyone talks to me in this certain reverential tone, like they're thinking all the time that I'm Sid Hughes's son, so they should be friendly and humor me and smile a lot. Maybe they think I've got an inside track to show business, or my dad's got a nice cushy job lined up for me on his talk show; but they're wrong. They look at me and see my dad, not me. I'm invisible—the same way I'm invisible to my dad. He sees what he wants to see, just like they do.

I go along with the whole charade, always polite and deferring, saying things like, "Yeah, Sid Hughes is the greatest," or "Sure, I'm a chip off the old block." But I feel more like a splinter. I don't like to make waves, so I just say what I figure they want me to say.

6

It's not hard. I've been doing it since I was five.

The truth is that I'm not my dad and never will be. But I think I'm the only one who knows that. I suppose I should speak up and let the world know I'm me—someone entirely different from Sid Hughes —but I've never been able to find the words. Besides, I'm not sure who I am. I keep trying to figure it out, but my mind keeps turning up blank. Empty. Or maybe I'm just chicken—a possibility that bothers me a lot and makes me feel guilty if I think about it too hard.

You see, my dad is this cool, strapping, smooth-talking guy who can walk into a room and take it over. His dark, shrewd eyes bore right through people, unnerving them. Everyone knows he's there—before he even says a word. He has this presence about him—a submerged sense of power and control. I've never seen him miss a beat or be at a loss for words. I'll never forget the day he interviewed the presidential candidates—the way he egged them on, baited them, and shaved them down to size. One nominee almost lost his cool and probably quite a few votes, but Dad showed him no mercy. I guess that's why Dad's got a reputation for being the most ruthless and controversial talk show host in the business. Several critics claim he makes all the others look like a bunch of milquetoasts.

Maybe that's why I get the uneasy feeling sometimes that I'm just another one of Dad's guests, not his son. But I wouldn't even make a very good guest. I don't have a flamboyant personality. I'm not a fascinating conversationalist. In fact, I don't like to talk much. I don't even have any burning commitment to some weird cause.

Not that I'm deliberately trying to put myself down.

Actually, I guess I'm an OK guy—tall and dark like my dad, but with my mom's finer facial features. I'm lean, but I work out with weights when I have time. And I'm one of the best on the Roosevelt High swim team, although I doubt if my dad has ever noticed.

Like now. I knew Dad wouldn't notice me as I entered the control room at the television studio. The crew was busy videotaping my dad's show. I stood for a minute and watched the cameramen rolling in for better angles while the technicians monitored several miniature TV screens on the control panel. The floor director and program manager stood off to one side, their heads bent as they conferred together. I slipped quietly past them and sat down.

Dad was interviewing some preacher—a stocky man with wispy hair and pale eyes. They were debating textbook censorship in the public schools. Religious people are Dad's favorite target, and he was in top form, giving the guy both barrels.

"I can't understand why you're so hung up about obscene language in school library books," said Dad, sitting back, his elbows spread roomily on the oval, plush blue couch. "You know, some of those books are best sellers!"

"Actually, the issue's not one-sided," replied the preacher. "Did you know that feminists in Illinois wouldn't even allow the word *lady* to appear in a sixth grade reader? Now isn't that hung up?"

Dad shifted his position. His strong jaw froze in an expression of disdain. He sounded a little defensive. "They just object to the traditional role of Mom cleaning the stove or changing the baby's diapers, that's all."

"So you're saying it's OK to show Dad changing

8

baby's diapers—no problem," persisted the preacher. "But don't show Mom doing it?"

"I didn't say that—," began Dad.

The preacher leaned forward intently. "We just want Christian parents to have the same rights as feminists or racial minorities to strike phrases from textbooks that belittle Jesus Christ or are morally offensive."

A technician signaled to the floor director and warned, "This guy's starting to look too smart for Sid."

The director nodded. "You're right. Sid's looking bad. Let's go into a commercial."

The floor director got the signal from the control booth and cued my dad, who was now desperately looking for a way out. "Thank you very much, pastor," Dad said through clenched teeth. He turned and smiled thinly into the camera. "We'll be right back with the Sid Hughes Show after these commercial messages."

The announcer's voice boomed, "Coming up on the next half hour of the Sid Hughes Show, it's dieting and ESP! Finding yourself through your next divorce! And meet a group of junior highers who've found fulfillment by going on strike against their parents!"

Meanwhile, Dad quickly unhooked his microphone and stormed into the control room. "Where'd you get that guy? He was trying to make me look like a chump!"

The program manager gripped Dad's shoulder reassuringly. "Come on, Sid. You threw that 'Bozo' preacher to the lions!"

I stood up and gave Dad a tentative grin. "Hi, Dad. How ya doing?"

As Dad spotted me, the angry lines in his face softened. With a slow, appraising smile, he came over and cuffed my arm lightly. "Straighten your shoulders, Tim," he said.

I did, quick-like. But I thought, *The only time I slouch is around you, Dad.*

"What's up, Tim? I wasn't expecting you here today."

"I know, Dad. But I've got this paper for career planning and I'm really stuck—"

"Homework, huh? Well, your mom's the writer in the family."

"Yeah, I know, but it's about what I want to be. I thought maybe you'd have some ideas . . ."

The program manager interrupted. "Sid, your next guest is ready."

"He better be an improvement over the last guy," snapped Dad.

"Dad, listen," I pressed. "I just need to talk to you for a few minutes."

He gave my hair a tousle. "Sure. I'll see you tonight. I'll try to get home before bedtime."

"Dad, that'll be too late—"

"Thirty seconds, Sid," announced the floor director.

"Dad, please—!"

With a vigorous wave, Dad turned and strode out of the control room. I felt a churning sensation low in my stomach. I wanted to follow him onto the set and make him listen to me. But, of course, I couldn't. This was his domain where he was king. I was just . . . his son—a guy who didn't even know what he wanted to be.

The program manager sidled over and smiled ingratiatingly. "Hey, Tim, your dad's a great guy. Someday you'll be just like him!"

"No, thanks," I muttered under my breath and stalked out of the studio.

I had to go see Marty. He was the only one I could turn to. You see, we've been best friends since first grade. Man, we've seen each other through measles and broken arms and stolen bikes. When the class bully beat me up in second grade, Marty was the one who came to my rescue and gave the bimbo a black eye. When Marty's favorite grandpa died, I made him go fishing with me instead of moping alone in his room. Marty's always been there for me, and I've tried to always be there for him.

So you can see why I was anxious to share my latest dilemma with him. I took the elevated train home, then hiked the half mile to Marty's. When he opened the door, I noticed his curly red hair was more tousled than usual, and his freckled face lacked its usual mischievous Huckleberry Finn animation.

"What's up?" I quizzed, hoping he would make it fast so I could spill out my problem.

"No big deal," he shot back. He sauntered outside and shut the door behind him. Marty's a tall, rangy, muscular guy with the prominent, irregular facial features of a young Abe Lincoln. And right now he looked as grim as some of those faded photos of Abe in my history book.

"Wanna take a hike?" I offered.

He nodded. We walked down the street away from his house. "Anything wrong?" I asked.

Marty was ambling along, his thumbs hooked on his jeans pockets. "Naw. It's just my folks." He tossed off the remark with his usual casual air.

I nodded. Marty's parents have a way of keeping things stirred up, but it never seems to phase Marty.

11

Over the years, whenever the battle got too loud or too fierce, Marty would camp out at my house for a few days. "So what's the fight about this time?" I asked.

"It ain't nothing. Just the same old thing—" he gave an exaggerated shrug "—my dad threatening to take a hike."

"Well, man, you've always got me," I said with a tentative grin.

Marty laughed and cuffed my shoulder playfully. "Man, how could I forget you?"

It was then, while we were shambling along laughing, that we spotted the ice cream truck.

2

Marty saw the truck first, parked beside the highway near the forest preserve that separates our neighborhoods. He nudged me and nodded toward the truck. "Hey, man, you hungry?"

We crouched down in the tall grass across the road from the truck. "I bet that thing's full of ice cream!" I whispered.

"Yeah, I sure could go for a bar or two!" exclaimed Marty.

We watched as a girl jogged up to the truck and spoke with the ice cream man—a runty, paunchy little guy wearing sunglasses, with stereo headphones in his ears. "Can I help you with something?" he asked the girl.

"I'd like a toasted almond bar, please."

"Sure. Hold on a second." He opened the little freezer door in the side of the truck and handed her a bar.

"Thank you," said the girl.

"I'd sure like to take a ride in that truck," Marty whispered.

"Don't think he'd take us. No room."

"I didn't mean with him." A sparkle was back in Marty's eyes.

"You crazy, man?" I asked, my hands growing clammy.

"You said you didn't know what you wanted to be," charged Marty. "Well, I wanna be a truck driver!"

"That's stealing," I stalled. I felt a sudden gnawing in my gut.

"No problem," Marty answered. "Look, the guy's walking away—over there by those bushes. Maybe he wants to have a smoke."

"Or take care of business."

"This is our chance," said Marty, standing up. "Come on, buddy. This is going to be a piece of cake!"

We darted across the road and gave the truck a quick once-over. "You sure you know how to run one of these things?" I asked.

"Yeah, sure, I watch 'em all the time!"

My heart was thumping like crazy. "All right, let's go!"

Marty jumped up into the cab of the truck and grabbed the keys from the dashboard.

"Hey, we got a whole thing full of ice cream!" I whistled.

Marty leaned over the steering wheel, looking frustrated as he hurriedly tried one key after another. "Man, these keys! This thing don't start! It's not turning over, Tim. Something's wrong!"

I craned my neck around the truck. "He's coming back, Marty. The dude's coming back!"

"What am I supposed to do?" Marty shot back.

"Give me some money. Give me some money, quick! Hurry up!"

The ice cream man ambled around the back of the truck toward me. I could tell he was all caught up in the music from his headphones, because he jumped a

14

little when he spotted me. "Yeah, do you need something?" he asked warily.

I leaned nonchalantly against the side of the truck and moved my lips, pretending to say something. The guy got the point and took off his headphones. "Sorry," he mumbled.

"Yeah, yeah. I was wondering if you could tell me exactly what a 'Jumbo Jet Star' consists of?"

He shrugged and said, "Sure. Pineapple, water, sugar. It's great on a warm day."

"All right, I'll have one of those, then."

"OK, fantastic." He opened the freezer door and bumped into me as I maneuvered myself around to hide Marty from his line of vision. "Excuse me," he murmured, and handed me the ice cream. "Here you go. I hope you enjoy it."

"OK, how much is that?" I asked, pretending to count my change.

"It's sixty-five cents."

"There you go, sir." I dropped a handful of pennies into his hand, making sure they missed and fell on the ground instead. "Sorry about that!"

"Dumb kid!" muttered the man as he stooped down to retrieve the coins.

The truck began to move. I scrambled into the cab beside Marty. "Go, man! Let's go! Go!"

Marty gunned the engine, and we peeled off down the road, leaving the pudgy ice cream man in the dust. I looked around breathlessly and saw the squat little dude chasing after us as fast as his short legs would carry him. He was hollering, "Hey, that's my truck! Come back with my truck!"

Marty was laughing so hard he could hardly grip the steering wheel. Gleefully he pressed the gas pedal all the way to the floor. We had that old truck sailing, man. I mean, we were really accelerating! The wheels sang, making that pavement sizzle. I could almost glimpse the shocked expressions of motorists and pedestrians as we whizzed past. For a few dizzying moments I felt powerful, like I could do anything, be anyone.

We tore through the forest preserve, down residential streets, and out onto the open highway, driving all the way to the beach. Like a kid with a new toy, I stood up and waved and rang the ice cream bell, making it clang for all it was worth. I tell you, that ride was a real trip to the moon!

Finally, Marty pulled to a stop on the packed beach sand. Still riding a wave of exhilaration, we both scrambled out of the cab and, taking turns with the bullhorn, shouted to the late-afternoon sunbathers, "Free ice cream, everybody! Everybody over here! Free ice cream!!"

They came from everywhere—little kids, guys and girls in swimsuits, some still wet from the water—and converged around the ice cream truck. Everyone was shouting at once. A dozen hands reached out, grasping for ice cream. "Give me a fudge bar! I want a snow cone! Popsicle here! Over here!"

We worked as fast as we could to accommodate the crowd, handing out ice cream right and left to the sea of eager hands.

"Here! Over here! Throw me a chocolate!" came a cacophony of voices. "Hold it! Hold it! I'll take one! I want chocolate!"

Marty and I were so busy passing out ice cream that we didn't realize the siren in the distance was for us. A white squad car pulled up behind the ice cream truck, and two police officers jumped out and bolted toward us. Their dark expressions told us they weren't just out selling tickets to the policeman's ball.

One officer shouted, "You two! Over here! Hands on the truck! Let's go! Get your hands on the truck!"

The crowd was reluctant to disperse. Everyone hung around watching in curious silence while Marty and I stood spread-eagled, suffering the humiliation of a body search.

One officer poked me. "What's your name, kid?"

"T-Tim Hughes," I croaked.

"What's your father's name?"

"S-Sid Hughes."

"Not *the* Sid Hughes—the guy on TV?" He shook his head, marveling. "Well, whaddaya know!"

As I slouched in the back seat of the patrol car, the thrill of our madcap ride was gone; my spirits felt as deflated as a punctured balloon. Then I thought about what my dad would say when I phoned him from the police station, and my mood really took a nose dive.

Sure enough, my dad was enraged, although I wasn't sure whether he was angry because Marty and I had stolen the ice cream truck or because his own pride was wounded. A celebrity's kid had been caught. People might suspect that there was a chink in the armor of the high and mighty Sid Hughes.

Since Marty and I were both minors, we were released to our parents' custody. But the juvenile court judge sentenced us to work the whole month of July for the ice cream company to pay back what we had given away at the beach. I never realized how hard those ice cream people worked to support themselves.

I knew what Marty and I had done was wrong. There was no getting around the fact that we were guilty of stealing. I just wanted to put the whole sordid experience out of my mind, but one evening late in July my parents sat me down to talk, and I realized they still had a lingering concern about my wayward behavior.

Mom was twisting a brochure in her hands. She's a neat lady with short blond hair, kind of slim and pretty—a mom with no wrinkles. But tonight for the first time I noticed worry lines around her eyes.

"What is it, Mom? What's on your mind?" I asked, nervously cracking my knuckles.

She handed me the brochure. I unfolded it and scanned the words, then looked up at Dad. He was sitting with his arms folded sternly, a dark scowl on his face.

"This is a brochure for a Christian summer camp, Dad," I said. "What's it all about?"

"Ask your mother," he snorted. "It's not my idea."

Mom seemed to be trying to convince Dad. "A Christian camp just might be the thing that turns him around, Sid. Look at the brochure. It's a perfectly good program. A full waterfront program, horseback riding, team sports—"

Dad glared at her. "I don't care if they have hang-gliding and deep sea fishing. I'm warning you, Meg, if you send Tim to a camp like that, he'll come back a born-again Bible banger."

Mom looked pleadingly at me. "How about it, Timmy? Would you like to go to camp? It'll only be for a couple of weeks."

I shifted uneasily. "You don't want me to go, Dad. Please," I said, grabbing at straws.

He wouldn't look at me. "No, I don't, but I don't want you getting into more trouble with Marty."

I felt betrayed. "You always liked Marty," I said accusingly. "Besides, we've done a good job at the ice cream company. Ask anybody."

"I know, but the job's over in August. It's not good for you to have too much time on your hands. Who knows? Maybe your mother's right."

"Sure, send me off to some dumb camp," I grumbled. "It'll keep me out of everyone's hair."

That weekend, when Marty and I went fishing at the riverbank, I told him about the camp I would be attending in August.

"A camp? What kind of camp?" Marty wanted to know.

"I don't know. It's just—you know—a camp," I said evasively.

"Come on! What kind of camp?"

"I don't know the name of it. It's in Wisconsin."

Marty laughed knowingly. "What's the story?"

"All right" I sighed relentingly. "My folks are sending me to this Christian camp because they think it's gonna shape up my behavior." I forced a chuckle. "Actually, I owe it all to you, buddy. If we hadn't taken off with that ice cream truck—"

"Your folks are still hanging that trip on you?"

"Aren't yours?"

"Naw. They ain't got time. They got other things on their minds."

"Well, the camp shouldn't be too bad," I remarked, trying to sound convincing. "There's some nice-looking girls on the brochure."

Marty gave me his Huck Finn grin and laughed scoffingly. "Man, I can see it now! Front page of the *National Enquirer*—'Sid Hughes's son attends Christian summer camp!'"

Marty was just being funny, but he didn't know the half of it. In fact, neither of us realized then that summer camp would change everything between us.

3

Cedar Ridge Camp turned out to be more than I ever imagined. I admit, at first I felt a little uneasy. I had this image of Christians in my mind—a bunch of losers sitting around with long faces. But they weren't like that at all. They were regular kids who liked having fun as much as anyone. We played volleyball, went canoeing and horseback-riding, rode the water slide and catamaran, swam and wind-surfed, and devoured the chow like we were afraid of starving.

During the evening firesides, kids got up and talked about Jesus like He was somebody real, someone who truly cared about them. They really seemed happy and content. But I was skeptical. I figured, like my dad always said, religion was a crutch for the weak—Pablum for the poor and downtrodden.

But the more I thought about it, the more I realized I needed something—call it a crutch or a cure, I wanted some meaning in my life. So when Jerry, my counselor, talked about Christ being the Way, the Truth, and the Life, deep inside I knew He was the one I needed. The idea of making a commitment to God's own Son really blew my mind. The beauty of it was that Jesus wasn't just laying down a bunch of rules and regulations; He had laid down His life because He loved me. I couldn't imagine anyone loving me that much. That's why, on the last day of camp, I prayed and asked Jesus to give me a new life in Him.

That evening, as a bunch of us guys sat around the campfire, I started to worry about what everyone back home was going to think. "I wonder what it's going to be like at school being a Christian," I said uneasily.

"Watch out for your old friends," warned one guy. "They're just gonna drag you down."

"Are there many Christians in your school?" asked Jerry.

I shrugged. "If there are, I've never heard of any. The only time you hear the Lord's name at Roosevelt High is as a curse word."

"Do you know of a good church you can attend?" Jerry questioned.

"I don't know any churches at all," I replied. "I've seen a couple, but you see, my parents aren't Christians, and I've never really been to church."

Jerry took a piece of paper from his pocket and wrote something down. "Look, Tim," he said. "Here's the name of a girl who goes to your school. Give her a call when you get home. I think she's active in a local youth group."

I nodded and tucked the paper in my wallet. I had a feeling I was going to need all the help I could get. In fact, I already had misgivings about what I was going to tell Mom and Dad when they picked me up at camp tomorrow.

Sure enough, when Dad pulled up in his big Lincoln the next afternoon, I still had mixed feelings. It was good to see them again, but I could already anticipate Dad's reaction to my becoming a Christian.

I waited until we were on our way home before bringing up the subject. Mom was her usual bubbly self, gushing about how I'd put on weight and gotten a great tan. "Look at him, Sid. Doesn't he look great?"

Dad looked over from the driver's seat and winked. "He's smiling about something."

Mom laughed and said cozily, "Maybe he's got a girl friend."

Dad gave a sly chuckle. "Probably doesn't want to talk about it."

I took a deep breath and plunged in. "Mom, Dad, I gotta tell you about the greatest thing that's ever happened to me."

Now Mom and Dad were really grinning!

"Uh-hm," said Dad, sounding convinced. "What's her name?"

Mom nudged Dad playfully. "Find out what he has to say, dear."

"Hey, Meg, I'm not stopping him."

"Well," I began, struggling for the right words, "I learned how the Bible says we're like sheep gone astray—"

"Oh, hey, that reminds me," interrupted Dad. "We got the wool blankets you liked. On sale at Kroyden's —you know—the plaid ones?"

"And the matching drapes," continued Mom uneasily. "I just know you'll love them!"

"Thanks. I appreciate it, Mom. Well, anyway—"

"Go on," said Dad warily.

"Yes, go ahead, Timmy," said Mom.

I sighed nervously. "What I'm trying to say is that I-I've become a Christian."

Dad stiffened, and his knuckles blanched as he gripped the steering wheel. "Wait a minute. Say that again?"

More quietly, I said, "I've become a Christian, Dad."

For a minute no one said a word. Then Mom managed to find her voice. "That's very interesting, Timmy. Thank you for sharing that with us."

Dad, shifting in his seat, forced a hollow-sounding laugh. "You did no such thing, Tim."

My voice was barely a whisper. "Yes, I did, Dad."

Mom came to the rescue. "Oh, look, Sid," she exclaimed. "There's McDonald's! Let's stop for Chicken McNuggets!"

But Dad wasn't about to be diverted. "Hold on, Meg. Wait a minute. I paid six hundred dollars to send my kid to summer camp so he can come back some religious nut?"

"I'm sure he did other things, too, dear," said Mom placatingly. "I can remember summer camp. Swimming, boating, tennis—maybe he even made some moccasins—"

"I just don't get it," interrupted Dad, growing angrier by the minute.

I slouched inconspicuously in my seat while Mom babbled on in my defense. "Well, maybe he's just expressing some emotional feelings like they have in those religious gatherings when they all sing out loud and—"

"You just don't make a big decision like that in one week," muttered Dad.

I winced inside. "Mom, Dad, it wasn't an emotional thing. Believe me, it's real."

Mom patted my hand reassuringly like she used to do when I skinned my knee. "Oh, Timmy, I'm sure that what you're saying is very sincere." After a moment, her voice brightened. "By the way, honey, Marty called. He's got a brand new car. He can't wait to take you for a ride in it."

I should have felt happy for Marty, but I didn't. He was another hurdle I had to face. How could I tell him about the decision I'd made to become a Christian? I could already hear him laughing uproariously. And how was I going to handle it when he expected me to resume some of our old pastimes, like drinking and smoking and partying?

It didn't take long to find out. Several days later he came by and picked me up for a ride in his new car—a red convertible, a real beauty. But he brought along a six-pack of beer to celebrate. As we sped along, I sat with the open can in my hand, wondering what to do with it. I sensed already that Jesus didn't want me drinking beer, but I didn't want to offend Marty. In desperation I tried to figure out how I could please them both.

Finally, when Marty wasn't looking, I held the can out the window and poured some beer over the side of the car.

"So how was camp?" Marty asked conversationally.

"It was really good."

"And how were the girls?"

"They were nice!"

"That's cool."

"So how does Debbie like your new car?" I asked.

"My lady likes what I like," said Marty proudly. He paused. "You know, I'm gonna put a set of chromes on."

"Great," I said, trying to sound enthusiastic.

Suddenly Marty noticed my sleight of hand with the beer can. "Hey, what are you doing, man?"

"Nothing," I said quickly. "I, uh, just got a hair in here." I blew at the can, then lamely shook my head.

"I don't know, Marty. This stuff tastes terrible."

"Ah, come on! You ain't even tasted it yet," he said sourly.

I just hung my head.

"Man, it's that camp!" he growled as he gunned the engine.

I sat back and heaved a sigh of frustration. So far my testimony for Jesus was a washout!

Things got even worse when the fall semester at Roosevelt High started two weeks later. I was a junior now, with harder classes and a heavier work load. But heaviest on my mind was the fact that so far—aside from that initial disaster with my parents—I hadn't taken a stand for Christ.

Then an unexpected opportunity came during Mrs. Buell's English class. Mrs. Buell, a short, thick-waisted woman with a tight, braided bun, was writing her name on the blackboard when I first entered the classroom. I sat down and glanced around. Most of the students were busy talking to one another, catching up on their summer activities. Some sat slumped in their seats. No one looked in the mood for academics. One guy was already defacing his new textbooks; another was listening to his Walk-Man, his head bobbing up and down to music only he could hear. Dennis, a mildly retarded student with blunt features and a bulky, loose-jointed frame, was struggling to copy Mrs. Buell's name in his notebook.

Just after the tardy bell rang, Marty swaggered in and sat down to the cheers of his classmates. I mean, he was given a real hero's welcome. "How ya doin', Marty?" someone called.

"Not bad, not bad." He grinned, lapping up the attention.

Mrs. Buell turned to the class and announced precisely, "That's Mrs. Buell, class, spelled B-U-E-L-L."

"B-U-E-L-L," blurted Dennis.

There was a ripple of coarse laughter across the room.

"All right, class," chided Mrs. Buell. She attempted to pick up her record book, but it was stuck to her desk. Everyone's eyes turned toward the glue bottle planted on Dennis's desk.

As Mrs. Buell walked down the aisle toward Dennis, the boy behind him hooted, "Oh, Dennis, you've been a bad boy! I'm gonna tell your mother about this!"

"I didn't do it," whined Dennis. "Somebody put it there!"

I caught a smirk on Marty's face as Mrs. Buell took the glue bottle and returned to the front of the room.

"All right, class, I have an assignment for you. I want you to write about what is the most important thing in the world to you."

The entire class roared in unison.

"Girls!" quipped Marty.

"Yeah, great, Marty!" someone agreed.

Mrs. Buell spoke above the din. "You are to write at least two paragraphs. The papers will be due first thing in class tomorrow."

For the next few minutes I didn't hear anything else that was said. I was thinking hard about the writing assignment. Yes, of course. I would title it "The Greatest Thing in the World to Me." This was my big chance to stand up for my faith. I knew I had to put things on the line. Either I'd speak up—or I'd have to lie. One thing for sure—this undercover stuff would have to come to an end!

4

That afternoon I was out playing on the soccer field when I spotted Marty driving up in his new car. I ran over to the parking lot and greeted him. "Hi, Marty! What's up?"

He climbed out and sauntered over to me. "Hey, man, how's it going?"

"What's happening?" I asked, nodding at the printed fliers in his hand.

"Check it out, man!" His face was beaming. "I just thought I'd stop by and let you know I'm running for class president again."

I laughed uneasily at the headline, "PARTY WITH MARTY! SCHOOL DEMAGOGUE PROMISES BIG REFORMS!"

"So what do you think?" he prompted.

I dodged the question. "What are you going to promise this year? Driving privileges for freshmen?"

"Nah-nah-nah! I'm gonna go with a completely different approach," said Marty slickly. "The fact is, deep down, everybody in school wants good times!"

"Oh, wow! Who's gonna fight against that?"

A troubled expression crossed Marty's face. "Wanna know who? This William McAllister the

Third character. He's all for school spirit and all that rot. He ain't got a chance though. We're gonna blow his doors off, me and you, Tim. All right?"

I gave him an accommodating nod. "All right."

Marty handed me several of the leaflets. I took them reluctantly. Already my conscience was starting to bother me. I no longer believed in all the things he would be promoting, but what could I do? He was my best friend.

"Hey, man, listen," urged Marty. "I'll pick you up tomorrow morning at seven fifteen, and we'll do some campaigning around school, all right?"

"Yeah, sure."

Marty tossed me an appreciative grin as he opened his car door. "Catch you later, buddy!"

I waved, then jogged back to my soccer game with Marty's fliers. My misgivings were growing by the minute.

At home that evening, I decided I had to do something about making some new Christian friends. That's when I remembered the phone number my counselor, Jerry, had given me at camp. I made the call after dinner while Mom and Dad were watching a presidential news conference on TV. As the President responded to a question about school prayer, Dad growled, "When politicians start talking about religion, then I've had it!"

I took the telephone out into the hallway and nervously dialed Becky's number. Finally, a girl's voice said, "Hello?"

In my most sincere tone, I asked, "May I speak to Becky Olson, please?"

"This is Becky," she replied expectantly.

"Hi. My name is Tim, and—"

"Tim Cameron?"

"No, ah—"

Brightly she asked, "Tim Elwell?"

"No, my name is Tim Hughes and—well, you don't know me, but—"

Her voice grew wary. "Didn't you used to hang around with Marty Sullivan last summer?"

"Yeah," I admitted uncomfortably.

"Oh, yeah," she snickered. "I thought so."

I was getting nervous now, but I pushed on anyway. "Listen, Becky, I went to Cedar Ridge Camp last summer, and my counselor said that you might be able to tell me about—" I lowered my voice. "—about a Christian group that I could get in with." I glanced into the living room at my parents. They were both looking my way.

"Oh, our youth group!" bubbled Becky. "Hey, listen, why don't you meet me in front of the school tomorrow, and I'll introduce you to some of the kids?"

"Yeah, OK. That'll be great. All right! Thanks a lot!"

I hung up the phone and started for the living room, but I could see that Mom and Dad were waiting for a full report, so I turned and went to my room instead. I spent the rest of the evening trying to write my English assignment on "The Most Important Thing in the World to Me: Jesus Christ." The only problem was that the only thing I could come up with was the title.

I sat back in frustration and gazed around my room. It was a neat room with giant posters on the walls, trophies and ribbons from my soccer club and swim team, a few pictures of old girlfriends, a neat stereo system, and my big tank of tropical fish.

I stared back at my desk where my open Bible sat, along with several crumpled drafts of the same assignment on "Girls," "Sports," and "Fishing." At the rate I was going, I wouldn't even have a paper to turn in. I turned my gaze absently to Marty's campaign fliers, the brochure from summer camp, and a pamphlet I'd picked up on reading the Bible in a year. But nothing inspired me or made this paper easier to write.

I was almost relieved when there was a light tap on my door. Mom entered with a questioning smile. "You busy, honey?"

I pushed the blank paper aside and shook my head. "Not really. Just homework. Sit down, Mom."

She glanced over at the fish tank. "How are your fish doing?"

I knew she hadn't come in to talk about my fish, but I played along. "They're OK. But no babies yet."

"That's too bad."

I turned the questions back on her. "How're you doing, Mom? Getting any writing done?"

I could tell she was pleased by my interest. "A little. I finished a new chapter."

"That's great! Did you tell Dad?"

Her gaze lowered. "No. He thinks it's all rather silly—"

"That you're writing a novel? Man, I can't even come up with two paragraphs for English!"

"A romance novel," corrected Mom. "Your dad thinks that romance is a waste of time."

I gave her a knowing glance. "You mean in books or real life?"

"Both!" she laughed softly, but I knew she didn't think it was the least bit funny. For a moment I felt sorry for Mom. She's so sensitive and gentle, I don't know how she holds her own against Dad. Come to think of it, I'm a lot like Mom myself. I'm basically quiet and laid back like she is and nowhere near so intense and ambitious as Dad. Mom and I are both quick to put the lid on things to neutralize confrontations with Dad. It's not easy though, because he thrives on controversy and confrontation.

"Timmy, did you hear me?"

I realized with a start that Mom had been talking to me. "I'm sorry, Mom, what'd you say?"

"I said—you met a new friend?" She sounded uneasy.

"A new friend?"

"The person you were just talking to."

"Oh, on the phone! That's the girl I was supposed to get in touch with after camp."

Mom sat down on the bed beside my desk. "I see," she said slowly. She looked over at my desktop. "Is that a Bible?"

I picked it up. "This? Yeah."

"You're taking it to school?"

"Yeah." I felt awkward, like I should be offering some explanation.

"Pretty brave move," remarked Mom. "Do you think anybody's going to see you with it?"

I smiled sheepishly and showed her the pocket in my notebook. "I'm putting it in here."

Mom held her breath for an instant, then said, "OK." She gazed around the room like she was looking for a cue. "Can I get you anything?"

I looked searchingly at her. "You're worried about me, aren't you?"

She smiled gently and patted my hand. "What are moms for?"

"You don't have to worry, Mom. Everything's all right." I struggled for the right words. "I'm still me—I'm still Tim."

Mom's voice was tender. "OK, if you say so."

I sighed. "You don't understand, do you?"

"I'm trying." She stood up and walked to the door. "Good night, honey."

"Good night, Mom."

After Mom left, I sat for awhile staring dreamily into my tropical fish tank. Somehow things seemed clearer to me now. I knew what I had to write for my English assignment. I picked up the blank paper and wrote decisively, "The greatest thing in the world to me is Jesus Christ."

5

I was dressed and ready for school earlier than usual the next morning. I took one final look at my completed English assignment and put it away, then tucked my Bible inside my notebook. I was about to leave my room when I heard a car horn honking in the driveway. *Marty was here to pick me up!*

I'd almost forgotten my promise to help him pass out fliers for his campaign. I sat down at my desk and shook my head. How could I, a Christian, promote his brand of partying?

I heard the doorbell downstairs, then Mom's voice saying, "Marty! Come on in. Tim'll be right down."

I was trapped. Marty would be hurt if I didn't help him now. I had no choice. I stood up and opened my door a crack, then remembered the snicker in Becky's voice over the phone when she asked if I hung around with Marty Sullivan.

"Tim!" Mom called from the foot of the stairs. "Hurry up! Marty's here!"

I hesitated. This was the day I would be meeting my new Christian friends. I couldn't let them see me associating with Marty. I opened my door and shouted downstairs, "Uh, Mom, could you tell Marty just to go ahead? I'm running a little late. I'll take the bus and see him at school."

I heard Marty quip, "He probably just woke up, the clown."

I stood in my bedroom doorway and listened sheepishly as Dad joined the conversation downstairs with Marty. "Hey, Marty, missed you around here lately!" he said. "Stop over for a beer sometime, why don't you?"

"Sidney!" scolded Mom.

"We'll celebrate when I get elected class president," Marty promised.

"Hey, it's in the bag!" exclaimed Dad. "Mr. Popularity, right?"

From my bedroom I listened to their conversation with a twinge of envy. Marty had a special rapport with my dad I'd probably never have. It had been that way since Marty and I were kids. He and my Dad were both strong-minded extroverts who made no bones about what they believed. As a new Christian, I wasn't sure I could accept what either of them stood for, but would I ever have their kind of courage to stand up for my own convictions?

After Marty left, I killed a few more minutes in my room. I couldn't believe how guilty I felt just for trying to do the right thing. Finally, I left my room, said a quick good-bye to my folks, and hurried off to catch the school bus.

But that bus ride didn't exactly turn out to be a picnic. In fact, I found myself wishing I'd caught a ride with Marty after all. Dennis Wetzel, the retarded student, sat across the aisle from me. Several of the guys behind him were getting their kicks by putting him down.

"Wow, Dennis, where did you get that outstanding book bag—at K-Mart?" teased one joker.

"A blue light special," sneered another guy. "One hundred percent pure artificial vinyl!"

"Hey, don't embarrass him," mocked a guy named Larry. "It says 'Recycled.'"

Dennis looked down at his bag. "No, it doesn't," he announced proudly. "It says 'Sears,' see? S-E-A-R-S. What's the matter? Can't you guy read?"

Everyone laughed and hooted. I wanted to turn around and tell them to knock it off, but I just couldn't force out the words. Instead, I clenched my teeth and looked the other way. I wondered, Why did those jerks have to get their laughs at someone else's expense? Maybe just as bad, why was I letting my own embarrassment keep me from sticking up for Dennis?

"It's OK, Dennis," someone was saying with fake sympathy. "Larry's had a severe reading problem since first grade."

"Yeah, that's right," replied Larry, playing along.

Sure enough, Dennis walked innocently into their trap. "Hey, Larry, I'll teach you how to read," he said earnestly. "I'm in the Bluebirds now in my special reading class."

"Oh, wow, the Bluebirds! Hear that, you guys—the Bluebirds!"

"Thanks anyway, Dennis," said Larry, leaning over the seat. He picked up Dennis's sack lunch and started rummaging through it. "This is some lunch you got here, Dennis."

"Yeah, my mother makes those for me. Tuna fish and bologna. My favorite."

"Tuna fish and—huh? Hey, look at this, fellas," said Larry with mock exaggeration. "There's a bug on here." He held the sandwich out the open window. "I'll shake it off for you, Dennis."

Dennis turned around and reached for the sandwich. "Hey, come on, man. That's my lunch."

Larry deliberately dropped the sandwich on the pavement. "Oh, whoops! Sorry about that."

I looked back and gave Larry a dirty look, but he didn't notice. He was too busy laughing at Dennis.

"Hey, driver, stop the bus!" Dennis shouted, waving his arms frantically. "I lost my lunch! Stop the bus!"

I glanced down sheepishly at my own lunch sack. I knew I should offer half my sandwich to Dennis, but I didn't want the guys laughing at me as well. So I stared out the window, trying to detach myself from the whole ugly mess. But this gal sitting with Dennis —Traci somebody, a sophomore—saved the day by giving Dennis her sandwich. Dennis, practically speechless with surprise, refused it at first, but Traci insisted. "I really want you to have it," she said, casting a piercing glance at Dennis's tormentors.

I settled back in my seat, thinking that the rest of the ride would be a piece of cake. But wouldn't you know? Without warning—almost as if it had a will of its own—my Bible worked its way out of my notebook and fell on the floor right in the middle of the aisle. I could feel my face growing hot as I bent down discreetly to retrieve it. Had anyone noticed? If Larry and his gang caught sight of me with a Bible, I'd be a dead pigeon.

Before I could pick up the Bible, Traci leaned over, snapped it up, and sat there examining it like she'd never seen anything like it in her life. "Oh, wow!" she exclaimed, her eyes wide with disbelief. "You bring this to school?"

I held out my hand and said quietly, "Can I have that back?"

She nodded so that her long brown hair sort of bounced around her shoulders. "You've got a lot of guts!" she said with awe. I wasn't sure whether she thought I was crazy or cool.

With a darting glance, I slipped the Bible back inside my notebook. The two guys behind me snickered, but I stared straight ahead, hoping the whole thing would blow over without anyone else knowing.

I was breathing a lot easier when the bus finally pulled to a stop in the school parking lot. As I stepped off, I silently congratulated myself. I had saved face and avoided any awkward confrontations with Marty, Larry, or any of the other guys. The rest of the day would be smooth sailing!

But I had spoken too soon. As I approached good old Roosevelt High, Marty, his girlfriend Debbie, and the rest of his gang pulled up in his red convertible like they were part of some presidential motorcade. A huge sign on the side of Marty's car read, "PARTY WITH MARTY!" A mob of students quickly gathered around, laughing, hooting, and cheering. I tried to step back behind someone, out of Marty's view, but he spotted me anyway.

Sitting on the back of his convertible like some sort of royalty, Marty flashed me the peace sign and grinned. He was wearing his Levi jacket and a rolled bandanna around his head. "Hey, Tim!" he called.

I waved back feebly. "Hi, Marty."

"You lazy bum! Can't you ever get up on time?"

"Sorry about that," I mumbled. "What are you guys doing?"

"Bummin' around, man," said a dude in a tee shirt with rolled sleeves.

"We're cruising around" replied Marty, "getting a little exposure for my campaign."

"Like P.R., man," said Debbie.

"Come aboard, Tim," Marty coaxed. "It's not every day you can hit the campaign trail like this."

"Yeah, I know," I said, glancing around, wondering if Becky and her friends had spotted me yet.

Several of the guys started speaking at once. "Hop on board, man! Come on, there's room. Let's go! Get in, Tim!"

Marty looked me straight in the eye. "Are you joining us, man, or not?"

I shifted my books uncomfortably. "I really can't right now. I gotta meet somebody."

The betrayed expression in Marty's eyes chilled me. He signaled to his driver. The guy gunned the engine and peeled away, leaving burnt rubber, exhaust fumes, and an ear-splitting screech in his wake.

I watched them drive away with a sinking sensation in the pit of my stomach. I had disappointed Marty again. But what was I supposed to do? I was trying to make Jesus my Lord, and I couldn't imagine Him approving of Marty's life-style. But the questions burned in my mind: What was I supposed to do with my non-Christian best buddy now that I was a Christian? Was I still supposed to consider Marty my friend but just not hang around with him anymore?

I was really confused that day, but I was about to meet someone who would give me a totally unexpected answer.

6

Becky Olsen was waiting for me at the front entrance of the school. At first I wasn't sure that this perky blonde with rosy cheeks and dimples was Becky, but I sure hoped so. She was just standing there in her angora sweater and designer jeans, looking around expectantly, so I ambled up bravely and said, "You gotta be Becky, right?"

She looked me over with these big baby blues and gushed, "You're Tim? Why, you look just like Scott Baio!"

I chuckled self-consciously and mumbled, "Yeah, that's what people say."

"Oh, wow, I honestly can't get over—"

A strapping football jock passed by and blew Becky a kiss. "Hey, babe, how's it going?"

Becky tittered lightly and pretended to be shocked. "Oh, Ted!" she clucked. I noticed the trace of a smirk on her face.

For a moment I thought maybe Becky had forgotten about me, she was so busy searching the faces in the crowd. But finally she glanced my way and tossed out an explanation. "I'm trying to find some of the kids in our youth group so you can meet them."

I made it a point to stay by her side. "Yeah, thanks." I wanted Becky to understand where I was coming from, so I said, "You know, Becky, it's been kinda tough for me to find some Christian kids to hang around—"

A girl with a frizzy hairdo and jangly earrings sashayed by and called, "Hey, Becky, how's it going?"

"Oh, hi, Jenny! What did you get on your chemistry test?"

"B-minus! What did you get?"

"It's a secret!"

"Isn't it always? See you later!"

I tried again. "Like I was saying, Becky, it's been kinda tough for me to find some Christian kids to hang around with. And besides, what do I do with my old friends, you know?"

"Oh, yeah, well, you just gotta play games with them," she said breathlessly, smiling. "Like, don't look at them. Pretend you're busy. Pretty soon they get the message and bug off."

"Maybe so, but I—"

Another of Becky's friends came along and said in a syrupy sweet voice, "Hi, Becky!"

Becky managed to match her honey tones. "Oh, hi, Lorrie! Are you and Scott back together yet?"

"No," Lorrie answered dreamily, "but Bruce Meyers just made a pass at me."

"Oh, wow! Hey, keep me posted, all right?" After a minute, Becky looked back at me, all business again. "You'll like our youth group, Tim. We've got lots of basketball players, football players, cheerleaders—you name it! So are you gonna come?"

"Yeah, it sounds great. Do you have many activities?"

"Activities?" she bubbled. "Why, we've got Wednesday night youth group on Wednesday. Crusaders on Thursday. Friday night special on Friday. Seekers plus sometimes a special activity on Saturdays. We've got Sunday youth group on Sunday, plus regular church on Sunday morning, plus young people's church on Sunday night. We've got volleyball on Monday and choir practice on Tuesday."

"Wow!" I exclaimed, duly impressed. "It sounds like you guys are pretty spiritual!"

"Sure are!"

I nodded wistfully. "I really want to start getting into the Bible."

"Well, sure, we do that too," said Becky accommodatingly.

Just then Dennis, the slow kid the guys teased on the bus, and Traci, who retrieved my Bible that same day, walked by and greeted Becky.

Scarcely glancing their way, Becky gave them a lethargic, "Hi there."

Dennis wasn't about to be so easily dismissed. "Hey, Becky," he chortled, brimming with enthusiasm. "You going to the car wash Saturday?"

Becky's voice was dripping with sarcasm. "No, Dennis. I'm going sledding."

With a confused, "Oh, OK. Bye," Dennis meandered on after Traci.

"Are they a part of your youth group?" I asked, remembering how Traci had generously given Dennis her sandwich.

"Yeah," said Becky shortly, "but they're not who I'm trying to find." She paused, looking around, then waved briskly. "There they are!"

As a group of young people approached us, Becky

went to meet them, her voice buoyant. "Hey, the gang has arrived! Hi, guys! How are you?" She glanced around and motioned me over. "You're all just in time to meet somebody. This is Tim Hughes."

Several girls said, "Hi, Tim . . . How's it going? . . . Hello!"

I smiled and tried to greet everyone.

Becky was still talking. "Tim used to hang around with Marty Sullivan. But he got saved last summer, and now he's looking for some new friends."

"Hey, great," said one guy.

"Welcome, Tim," said another.

Then a tall, dark-haired preppy stepped forward and stared down skeptically at me. "Your dad's that secular humanist on TV, right?"

Immediately, I recognized William McAllister the Third. "Yeah," I said, my defenses rising.

Becky clasped my arm excitedly. "You're—Sid Hughes is your dad? Oh, my goodness! I don't believe it! *The* Sid Hughes!"

"Where have you been, Becky?" teased one of the guys.

William McAllister the Third studied me with an arrogance that made me want to punch him. "I watched your dad last Thursday," he drawled, "cutting down this lady who wouldn't pull the plug on her eighty-six-year-old father."

"Yeah, uh—" I began.

"This is Bill," said Becky, her voice oozing with admiration. "He's going to be our next class president."

"I'm not so sure," murmured Bill. His modesty was as fake as a three-dollar bill, but he obviously had Becky fooled.

"You're just being modest," she gushed. "Are you

44

all ready for the big speech first period?"

"Not really," he said, his tone somber. "I have to miss calculus."

Becky laughed brightly. "You're hilarious, Bill, you know that?"

I started to walk on ahead, but Becky caught up with me and urged, "Come on, Tim. You wanna walk me to the auditorium? They'll be giving the election speeches in junior class assembly. I can't wait to hear Bill."

"Yeah, me too," I agreed. "It should be one of those once-in-a-lifetime experiences." I glanced at Becky and shrugged. My sarcasm had missed her by a mile.

In the auditorium, I sat with Becky and her youth group. I felt a little awkward at first, especially when Marty got up to give his speech. I started to applaud vigorously, then realized that no one around me was clapping.

Still, Marty was in top form. "If I am elected as your next class president," he intoned, "my administration will bring to this school a new era of—" he paused meaningfully "—good times!"

There was enthusiastic applause from everyone except our little section of the auditorium.

"Also," continued Marty, "from now on, the speed limit in the student parking lot's gonna be thirty-five miles an hour!"

More applause, along with whistles and cat calls.

Marty was riding high now. "I promise to end the school dress code . . ."

"What a total jerk!" Becky whispered in disgust. "I can't believe it!"

". . . Except for you preppies, you can still wear your 'Izod' shirts and topsiders."

I glanced around. All the jocks and greasers were hooting and stomping.

"Finally," said Marty, his spirits obviously sailing, "in spite of the good-looking girls and extracurricular activities here at Roosevelt, let's face it—school's boring! If I'm elected, I promise a fifty percent increase in school parties."

Becky leaned over and whispered in my ear, "Did you hear what Marty did last summer?"

"No, what's that?"

"He went down to Miami to buy all these drugs to sell to the grade school kids."

I didn't reply. I just sat back uneasily and pretended to listen to Marty's speech. I knew Marty better than anyone, and I'd never heard anything about Miami. If the story was true, Becky knew something I didn't. If it wasn't true, she was sure doing her part to spread a nasty rumor. I knew I should have defended Marty, but—

"So, remember," Marty was saying, "when you go to the polls today, 'party' rhymes with 'Marty,' so vote for Marty Sullivan for junior class president. Thank you, all!"

There was a tumultuous round of applause, with dozens of guys and girls chanting, "Party with Marty . . . Party with Marty!"

Becky and her friends still weren't clapping, so neither did I. To be honest, I felt like a traitor!

Mr. Sherwood, the principal, stepped uneasily to the platform and raised his hands in a gesture of silence. He received some scattered booing, but after a minute the class grew quiet. "Now I would like to introduce the next candidate for president of the junior class," he announced, smiling warmly at Bill. "Scho-

lar, athlete, holder of many awards of distinction—
William McAllister the Third!"

Becky and her friends applauded enthusiastically,
but otherwise the response was lukewarm at best. I
hadn't planned to clap for good old William the Third,
but Becky gave me a scathing glance, so I obliged half-
heartedly.

In his usual pompous tone, Bill said, "Thank you,
Mr. Sherwood. Faculty. Members of the junior class.
As vandalism in our school increases, as the drug
problem runs rampant—" his self-righteous fervor was
at an all-time high "—we need a candidate who can
revive our sense of school spirit and personal
dignity."

Becky clapped loudly. Dozens of students groaned
and booed. Several wadded candy wrappers hit the
platform while a paper airplane wafted gently over
Bill's head.

Bill seemed oblivious to it all. "We have a candidate
in our midst who has promised us the moon," he continued loftily. "But is there a reasonable person here
who believes he will deliver?" Bill glanced conde-
scendingly in Marty's direction. "I think most of you
realize the gentleman sitting by me on this platform is
not the same man he was several months ago. A trip to
the local police station will tell you the whole story."

A ripple of murmurings rose from the audience. I
sat forward and stared intently at Marty. He was
laughing, but I could tell he was infuriated by Bill's
mud-slinging.

Unfortunately, William the Pompous didn't know
when to stop. "Do you want a class president with a
criminal record?" he challenged smugly, "or a proven
leadership record in this school's sports, academics,

and student government programs? I trust today when you go to the polls, you will make the right decision. Thank you!"

The audience—a fickle lot—applauded as wildly now for Bill as they had for Marty. But at the moment I wasn't aware of anything in that auditorium except the dark, wounded expression in Marty's eyes. I ached for Marty, and for myself as well. Through all our years of friendship, Marty and I had always been there for each other. Now, when Marty needed me most, I wasn't sure I could ever be there for him again.

7

I was dreading Mrs. Buell's English class that afternoon. I knew I'd have to face Marty, and I'd have to turn in my English assignment on the most important thing in the world to me.

When I entered the classroom, there was the usual pandemonium before the tardy bell. But it was nothing compared to the uproarious cheers that greeted Marty when he swaggered in a minute later. He went around clasping hands and accepting congratulations like a seasoned politician. And the election results weren't even in yet! But, by the response from everyone, I figured Marty had to be a shoo-in for class president.

As I took my seat, Mrs. Buell removed her reading glasses and raised her hand to quiet the class. "All right, students, I'm sure we're all very anxious to hear the results of the voting. There should be an announcement any minute."

"We know who won!" someone shouted.

"Yeah, party with Marty!" several students chorused.

"All right, class," said Mrs. Buell, more sternly, "please take out your papers on 'The Most Important

Thing in the World to Me.' We're going to read some of them out loud in class." She smiled encouragingly as she added, "Let's hear what some of you have written."

I shrank down in my seat, wishing I could become invisible. I hadn't planned on reading this assignment out loud. I took out my paper and scanned it again: "The most important thing in the world to me is Jesus Christ. Last summer I accepted Christ into my heart at camp. This decision has changed my life completely. I realize now what my purpose in life is—to serve Jesus Christ!"

I shook my head in dismay. Man, there was no way on earth I could read that paper to the class. They'd laugh me out the door for sure. I tore the paper from my notebook and crumpled it before anyone could see it. In panic, I began rewriting the assignment, this time on 'religion.' No, that was no good either. I crumpled that paper too.

Mrs. Buell was already calling on students. I could be next, and now I had no paper at all to read!

"Lorrie?" said Mrs. Buell.

Lorrie stood up and announced in her usual gushing tone, "I wrote about my pom-pom activities." Breathily, she read, "I have been on the squad for the entire last year, and I have obviously fulfilled my goal for this year too—"

Everyone groaned.

"Thank you, Lorrie. That's enough," interrupted Mrs. Buell.

"Mr. Dennis Wetzel?" she said kindly. "Would you like to read your paper for us, please?"

Dennis stood up awkwardly, his face flushing with embarrassment. He pushed his glasses up on his nose and glanced around cautiously. Stuttering, he read, "The most important thing in the world to me are animals. My favorite things in the whole world are animals. Because they are very, very curious of what we do, and I—"

"Thank you, Dennis," said Mrs. Buell. Dennis sat down with relief as Mrs. Buell turned to Marty. "Mr. Sullivan?"

Marty looked up passively and grunted, "Huh?"

"Would you kindly read your paper for us—and please stand up?"

I could tell Mrs. Buell's patience was growing thin. She was probably lamenting that there wasn't a Hemingway among the bunch of us. But at least everyone else had a paper to read. Staring down at my empty notebook page, I felt my panic rising like a boiling thermometer. I had to write something—anything!—but my mind was totally blank.

Marty stood up, leaning casually on one leg, and read, "The most important thing in the world to me: Going on vacations, getting away from school, partying with my friends, nice girls, fast cars, palm trees, and sand. I like to surf, so maybe it's good waves. I don't know; it's a tough question!"

Marty's paper sparked a flash of inspiration. Sure! Vacations! I began scribbling frantically.

I had written only a couple of words when Mrs. Buell called on me. "Tim, do you have something you'd like to share with us?"

A couple of my classmates had noticed me tearing up my assignment. They snickered now as I stared up wordlessly at Mrs. Buell.

"What's your topic, Timothy?" she persisted.

I shifted uncomfortably. "It's really not that good."

"Come on, Tim," goaded the guy behind me.

"Yeah, come on, Tim. Read it," chorused the rest of the class.

Mrs. Buell eyed me sternly. "Tim, would you like to read your paper for us?"

"Yeah, it should be real interesting," mused Marty sarcastically.

"Tim! Tim! Let's go, Tim!" several class members chanted impatiently.

Mrs. Buell was scowling now. I had no choice. Standing up nervously, I held my blank paper so no one could see it. With what I hoped was a relaxed smile, I pretended to read. "Vacations," I said brightly. "Why they are so important." I knew my voice sounded singsong as I rattled on, pulling thoughts from the air. "Vacations are a very necessary part of life. Without them life would get very boring. Vacations give your mind and body a break from the routine of life. They give your body a rest." I stopped and looked around sheepishly. "That's all."

The class hooted and laughed, apparently pleased that my paper was as average and uninspiring as everyone else's. I had been accepted without fanfare for a paper that didn't even exist!

I sat down, breathing a sigh of relief, and began to write my paper for real.

Mrs. Buell, knowing I was capable of better work, remarked, "That's rather minimal, Tim."

Before she could pursue the matter, a student messenger entered the room and handed her a slip of paper. The class really started to buzz now. It had to be the election results!

"Oh, class," declared Mrs. Buell pleasantly, "we have an announcement that you've all been waiting for."

A couple of guys slapped Marty on the back, congratulating him in advance.

Mrs. Buell waited until there was dead silence, then announced, "Bill McAllister has just been elected our new junior class president—"

I glanced quickly at Marty. His grin flip-flopped into a grimace, and he averted his eyes as the color drained from his face. He couldn't have looked more surprised and betrayed if he'd been stabbed with a knife.

"And Marty Sullivan," continued Mrs. Buell, "with the second largest number of votes, is our new vice-president."

Everyone was murmuring at once, shocked that Marty hadn't won. I wanted to say something to him, but the words just wouldn't come. We stared at each other. He rolled his eyes, as if to say, "So what?" But his gaze lingered a moment longer, and for just an instant I saw the hurt and vulnerability I knew he didn't want anyone else to see.

Mrs. Buell was still speaking. "Please pass your papers to the front of the class." As the dismissal bell rang, I scribbled the final sentence of my paper on vacations. The class was still boisterously debating the election results.

After class I followed Marty into the washroom. He needed someone now. I had to see if there was anything I could do to help. Marty was bending over the sink, splashing cold water on his face. I couldn't help wondering if he was trying to cover up his tears.

I leaned against the wall and looked earnestly at him. "Sorry about the election, Marty."

He stared straight ahead into the mirror as the water ran off his face. "Criminal record," he muttered, spitting into the sink. "Man, I ain't got no criminal record!

I'm gonna kick that fairy's head in right in front of his friends. Man, he's gonna be dead!"

After a moment, Marty looked over at me and seemed to brighten. "Hey, you wanna help me flatten him?"

I felt as if I had been practicing my answer for weeks, and I delivered it properly and antiseptically. Becky would have been proud of me, but I felt like a heel. "I'm sorry, Marty, I can't. I already got plans, you know?"

He looked down, shaking his head ponderously. "Ah, you don't wanna get involved in this kind of stuff no more, do you?"

When I didn't reply, Marty gave me a twisted grin and said, "Hey, how about going fishing with your old pal, Marty, huh? We haven't done much since you went up to that church camp."

I was feeling more miserable by the minute. I never should have thought I could help Marty now. "I got a lot going this weekend," I said evasively. "I'm sorry."

Something changed in Marty's expression then. His eyes turned stone cold, like he was dropping a curtain between himself and me. Or erecting a wall. The disappointment was thick in his voice. "Later, OK?" he said, and sauntered out without a backward glance.

"Yeah," I mumbled lamely. I couldn't have felt worse if Marty had punched me in the stomach.

8

That evening my dad was home early for a change. To celebrate, my mother suggested we play a game of "Life" after dinner. Dad thrives on those games, and he always wins. I agreed half-heartedly; at least it beat doing homework.

Halfway through the game, I realized I was winning. Somehow, it didn't feel right. I couldn't imagine my dad—the great Sid Hughes—losing to anyone, especially his own son.

"Revenge!" I quipped uneasily.

"Sue me, kiddo," said Dad gruffly. "You got the game."

"I don't want to sue anybody. I'll pass."

"You can't pass!" said Dad.

"Well, he doesn't have to sue," said Mom protectively.

"I'll send you back ten spaces then," I told Dad.

"That camp's taken all the guts out of my kid," Dad muttered.

I decided to steer the conversation away from potentially dangerous ground. "I met some new kids today at school," I remarked casually. "They invited me to their church car wash this weekend."

"Oh, I think that's wonderful," said Mom, obviously trying to make up for Dad's usual lack of enthusiasm.

He raised one eyebrow skeptically and grunted, "What's so wonderful about a car wash?"

I tried another tactic. "Would it be okay if I went with them on a retreat to Leech Lake next month?"

Dad dropped his play money. "What?"

"Leech Lake?" tittered Mom, amused.

Dad's brow furrowed. "It sounds like something out of the Dark Ages!"

Mom sounded interested. "What do they do at this—this retreat, or whatever you call it?"

"They lock you in a cell," snapped Dad sarcastically, "shave your head, and make you kneel on Uncle Ben's Converted Rice!"

"Sidney!" Mom scolded.

"We're going to go whitewater canoeing up there," I explained evenly.

"Oh, that sounds wonderful!" exclaimed Mom.

I smiled inwardly. Mom was always pulling for me.

"You can practice your J-stroke, Tim," she continued eagerly. "I think that sounds all right, don't you, Sid?"

Dad shook his head in disgust. "Meg, you're so trusting! We don't even know these people. This could be a cult or something."

Mom and I looked at each other, then we both looked at Dad. I think he figured he was in deep trouble with Mom if he didn't give in.

Throwing his hands up in frustration, he boomed, "OK, let the kid get cloistered on some Jim Jones weekend on some Leech Lake and come back a religious freak! That'll be just great!"

Mom and I exchanged congratulatory smiles, knowing this was Dad's way of saying yes. Concessions like this from Dad were unheard of in our family, and I knew enough to tread cautiously for the rest of the evening. I was about to tell Dad thanks, but he was busy taking another spin. "What'd you get?" I asked.

His eyes narrowed menacingly. "I just inherited fifty cats from my aunt, and I've got to pay twenty thousand dollars!"

Mom and I did our absolute best not to laugh.

That evening was a first in more ways than one. Not only did Dad lose our game of "Life" and give in to the canoe trip, but I successfully stood up for something I believed in that I knew Dad disapproved of. I've always given in to my dad, so it felt good to assert myself for a change. I wasn't fooling myself though. I knew that standing up for my new faith in Christ was going to be the challenge of my life, especially in the shadow of such an overpowering personality as my father's.

But at the moment I had other things to think about besides my dad. Actually, I spent most of the week thinking about the car wash on Saturday. I knew it was just another activity for most of the kids, but for me it would be my first opportunity to get acquainted with my new Christian friends. I still felt bad about Marty, but I tried to push the guilt feelings out of my mind. Marty knew I had chosen the car wash over a fishing trip with him, and he jibed me about it a few times that week. I told him he should join us and get to know these kids too, but he only hooted and did a comical imitation of William McAllister the Third. Finally, though, he got a sly gleam in his eyes and said he just might put in an appearance after all.

I figured he was joking, so I forgot all about his re-mark until the day of the car wash. The youth group met early Saturday morning in the church parking lot, and, man, did we ever have a lot of cars to wash! Everyone was working hard and having a great old time.

I met Steve, the youth pastor, a down-to-earth guy in his twenties, who greeted me with a hearty, "Glad you could be with us today, Tim."

"Thanks," I said, and added tentatively, "I've been really trying to find some new fellowship. You see, my dad and mom aren't exactly Christians—"

Before I could finish, several guys arrived with pota-to chips and soda pop. "Hey, Steve, where do we put this stuff?" they wanted to know. He shrugged help-lessly at me and led them off to the refreshment table.

I wandered over to a red VW that Bill McAllister and a guy named Ron were washing while they debat-ed theology. Bill might as well have been spouting a foreign language for all I understood of his bombastic blarney. "The Heidelburg and Westminster cate-chisms are an empirical manifestation by theologians of their attempt to put their Christian beliefs into a systematic situation of non-situational ethics," he in-toned loudly. "But, Ron, you're trying to say that they're some kind of formula—"

"I'm not saying they were a formula," protested Ron hotly. "I'm saying if you say that, then you're becom-ing a law-keeper, and the gospel is no longer central to the Christian experience."

"I'm not saying that," argued Bill. "That's the same hole you tried to put me in when you used your post-millennial literalism to duck end-times Bible prophecy."

By now, several of the guys and gals were snickering.

"Hey, you guys are giving me a headache!" declared Becky. On impulse she took the hose from the Buick she was washing and squirted Bill and Ron, drowning their argument for good. A gale of laughter rose from the group as the two drenched pundits sputtered and stammered and finally grabbed the hose, turning it back on Becky and the others.

In spite of all the hoopla and shenanigans, we managed to wash quite a few cars. By noon, our cash box was overflowing, so Steve put the money inside the church office for safekeeping.

When we finally broke for lunch, Becky and I, Bill and Ron, and a couple of others sat on the church steps with our sandwiches, chips and Cokes. I noticed two clipboards with sign-up sheets circulating. "Are those something I should be signing?" I asked.

"One is the whitewater retreat," said Becky cozily. "I already put your name down—beside mine."

"Practically everyone in the group has signed up," said Ron eagerly.

"Hey, that's great," I said.

Someone handed Bill the other clipboard. He looked at it and frowned. "Hey, this nursing home inner city sign-up thing has gone around three times and there are only two signatures on it."

"My parents don't want me going to the inner city," said Ron.

Bill nodded in agreement. "I make a motion we give this a decent burial."

"I second the motion," said Becky.

"All in favor, say, 'Aye.' "

In unison, everyone said, "Aye!"

"Motion carried," said Bill with a grin.

As Becky and I returned to the parking lot, I noticed Dennis and Traci working on a car together. Traci waved and said shyly, "Tim, Dennis and I are starting a new Bible study group at Roosevelt High. Can you come?"

Before I could answer, Becky interrupted coolly. "Look at all the cars lined up, Traci. We've got a ton of work to do. You and Tim will have to chat later." As we walked on, Becky whispered confidentially, "I can't believe it. Traci actually likes hanging around with retards."

"One thing you gotta say for Dennis," I murmured lamely. "He's got a real generous nature."

"Why not?" countered Becky. "What does he have to share?"

I squirmed inside, thinking there was more I should say in Dennis's defense and wondering why I should feel I had to defend him at all.

Becky and I had just started washing a new Chevy when I spotted Marty's red convertible squealing into the parking lot. Strange thing, though. Marty wasn't in the car. His tough gang buddies were piled inside, several riding the back and fenders like they were in some sort of weird parade. They peeled over beside us, burning rubber, and circled our group several times, tossing firecrackers at our feet.

"Hey, geeks! You turkeys!" they taunted as the firecrackers exploded noisily in flashes of fiery sparks, sending streams of foul-smelling smoke into the air. It looked, sounded, and smelled like the Fourth of July, but we weren't in the mood to celebrate. In fact, Bill, Ron, and some of the other guys looked like they were ready to fight. Finally, the rowdies screeched to a stop just inches from the car Becky and I were washing. They were still hurling insults. "You good little church kids having a nice time?"

Steve stepped forward and said, "Can we do something for you guys?"

"We just figured we'd see how you holy Joes spend your time," said the husky blond driver.

Ron leaned over to Steve and said, loudly enough for everyone to hear, "I'm going inside to call the police!"

Marty's driver picked up on Ron's threat. "Call the police?" His voice dripped with sarcasm. "Oh, yeah, that would be the Christian thing to do!"

"What would you know about it?" countered one of our guys.

"Oh, that sounds so religious," mocked the blond dude. "By the way, what are you planning to do with all that money you're making today?"

"It's none of your business," said Becky haughtily, "but we're going on a canoe trip."

Several of Marty's guys reacted to that one. "Oo-oo-oh! A canoe trip," a long-haired tough trilled as he pantomimed waves with his hands.

Bill McAllister stepped angrily toward the car. "You rowdies get out of—"

Immediately the blond leader growled, "Away from the car! Away from the car!"

"Yeah, let the goody two-shoes wash their cars and raise their money!"

"At least we're doing something constructive!" Bill shot back. "That's more than you guys can say for yourselves!"

The blond driver whistled through his teeth. "Hey, that's OK! We do things *de*-structive!" Everyone in

Marty's car cheered raucously.

Steve, the youth leader, made another attempt to defuse the situation. "Hey, you guys, we're trying to wash cars here. If you want to help us, grab a rag, huh?"

"Is that what you're doing? Wash our car then!"

"Yeah, go right ahead. Wash ours!"

"Let's go," ordered Steve. "Come on. Break it up!"

I stayed out of the whole thing. I still considered myself loyal enough to Marty that I wasn't going to tangle with his gang. But I was sure wondering where Marty was. I couldn't believe he would want his buddies heckling us like this. Only he could put a lid on this whole thing, and he was nowhere in sight.

Ron returned from the church building, and I heard Steve ask, "Did you call the police?"

"They're on their way," replied Ron vengefully.

The blond leader didn't hear that conversation. He was busy signaling Bill McAllister over to the driver's side of the convertible. "I've got a message for ya, mister," he drawled.

"Yeah? What's that?" said Bill.

"Somebody wants to give you some compliments for those kind words you said about him at the election assembly."

"Yeah, for sure!" echoed several gang members.

"What is it?" asked Bill warily.

The blond dude pulled out a raw egg and smashed it all over Bill's face. Bill stumbled backward, stunned, waving his hands in the air as if he had been blinded. Somehow, it struck me funny seeing the great William McAllister the Third, literally with egg on his face! I stifled my smile and ducked just as an egg sailed over my head. Suddenly, raw eggs were flying everywhere as Marty's gang pelted us like bombardiers over enemy terrain.

Becky managed to turn the hose on them, so they gunned the engine and tore out of the parking lot, shouting obscenities and insults

Just when I thought things were going to get back to normal, someone spotted Marty on the church fire escape.

"Look! He's got our cash box!" shouted Ron.

"That dirty thief!" exclaimed Bill. "He was using his gang to divert our attention!"

Bill and Ron took off after Marty as he leaped off the fire escape and sprinted through the parking lot with the steel box under his arm.

I was too stunned to move. Marty had done a lot of crazy things before, but he had never pulled a stunt like this one.

Bill and Ron wasted no time in nailing Marty and wrestling him to the ground. I had a feeling they planned to beat the tar out of him, but Steve intervened. "Hey, come on, you guys! Fighting's not going to solve anything!"

Bill and Ron weren't listening. They were punching Marty hard, venting all the anger his gang had stirred up with their raw eggs and insults.

"Let him go! Break it up!" shouted Steve.

I ran over and pulled Ron off Marty while Steve gripped Bill by the shoulders and yanked him back. "That's it! Break it up! Back off! Back off!" Steve ordered.

When Marty started to get up, Steve barked, "Stay down! You're not going anywhere. Hey, easy, man. Easy!"

I stared down at Marty lying bloodied and dirty on

the pavement. A sob rose in my throat that I could barely choke back. I wanted to reach out, say something, but the words wouldn't come.

Marty spat blood and wiped the side of his mouth. He turned away with the same remote glare of betrayal I'd seen when we talked in the washroom. I knew then that what had happened today had nothing to do with Marty's gang, or my new youth group, or even the election. It had to do with Marty and me. Setting up his friends to harass us, stealing, letting himself get caught—I could see that my friendship with Marty meant a lot more to him than I realized.

A siren sounded in the distance, and moments later a police car pulled into the parking lot. Two officers bolted from the vehicle and darted toward Marty. "What's going on here?" one demanded.

"He stole our money for the retreat!" cried Becky.

"Sullivan? You again?" muttered the other patrolman. He frisked Marty, then pulled his wrists behind his back and handcuffed him. "Looks like we got a lot to talk to you about down at the station."

The other officer gestured toward Steve. "Mind coming with us? We'd better hear the whole story."

I watched in surprise as Traci stepped forward and cautiously touched Marty's arm. "I'm sorry," she murmured. "Some of us really do care, Marty—but we don't know how to show it—"

Marty turned away bitterly, glanced back at me, then climbed into the squad car.

Becky came over, swinging her blonde hair breezily, and clasped my arm with a smug possessiveness. "I hope that jerk gets just what he deserves, don't you, Tim?" she cooed.

I shook her off and stalked away, before something I hadn't even known I felt inside exploded.

9

I didn't see Marty again for over a week. I tried calling him on the phone, but no one answered. Nobody at school knew where Marty was or what had happened. When I stopped by his house on Saturday, a week after the car wash, the place looked empty. Either Marty wasn't home or he was refusing to answer the door.

Then, the following Monday, while Mrs. Buell was passing back our English tests, Marty's name came up. "Does anyone know where Marty Sullivan is?" she asked. "He's been absent from class for an entire week now."

When she looked questioningly at me, I shrugged helplessly. Marty was my best friend—once. I should have known where he was. But I didn't.

"He probably overdosed," joked one of the guys.

"Or shot someone," snickered the dude behind me.

"Shot himself!" suggested Ron.

The whole class was murmuring now, speculating about Marty's activities and whereabouts. "Maybe he's in the slammer."

"I heard he got in trouble at the church over on Adams."

"I bet he's in the hospital."

"Naw. He beat it to Mexico for more drugs!"

"All right, class," said Mrs. Buell firmly. "Let's get started with our homework."

We all took out our papers as Mrs. Buell continued. "I'm asking you, in your opinion, what is the greatest writing in world literature?"

Everyone looked around blankly. One girl ventured, "*The Red Badge of Courage*, by Stephen Crane?"

"Anyone else?" asked Mrs. Buell.

"*Curious George?*" quipped one of the guys. Everyone laughed.

Mrs. Buell smiled knowingly. "Would you say that this is an adult—"

"Man, it's high-quality reading!"

"Oh, yes, certainly!" Mrs. Buell looked at me. "Tim?"

I was caught off guard. I shifted nervously, wanting to say, the Bible. It was more than just a book. It had the answer to life—Jesus—that everyone needed. As the word "Bible" formed in my mouth, my hands grew clammy, and my heart raced. But when it came right down to it, I wanted to look good in front of my classmates. I didn't want them pegging me as some Holy Joe type. So I managed a hapless grin and murmured, "Uh—I don't know. I haven't read that many books."

I could see that Mrs. Buell was disappointed by my answer. "There are a number of books on the desk that you could use for a reference," she said with a note of resignation.

Just then, Marty shuffled in, looking beat and bedraggled. The entire class grew silent as all eyes turned his way. I couldn't believe how bad Marty looked. His eyes were bloodshot, his clothes and hair a mess. He had lost weight. "Sorry. I overslept," he mumbled.

I felt a sudden impulse to jump up, grip Marty's arm and demand, *What's happening to you, buddy?* But this wasn't the time or place to confront him. I would just make us both look foolish.

"Marty, please come to the desk," said Mrs. Buell.

"Who paid your bail, Marty?" the guy behind me taunted.

I turned around and gave him a dirty look.

Marty trudged sullenly to the front of the room, his head lowered, his eyes downcast.

"You have these assignments missing in addition to the ones given out in class today," explained Mrs. Buell. "I suggest you get someone to tutor you."

Without a word, Marty took the mimeographed pages and shambled defeatedly to his seat.

"Perhaps there's someone who would like to help him with his homework," suggested Mrs. Buell. I had the feeling she was looking right at me.

I considered offering to tutor him. It would be the Christian thing to do. But would Marty take help from me now?

Before I could respond, Dennis raised his hand and said earnestly, "Mrs. Buell, I'd like to help him."

Several guys reacted with chuckles, smirks, and derogatory comments. "Yeah, Marty, Dennis will help you a whole lot. He's got it right up here, you know?" said one smart aleck, tapping his head.

Marty gave the guy a withering glance.

"Thank you for your kind offer, Dennis," said Mrs. Buell quickly. She gazed at Marty with concern. "Martin, I suggest you come in after school and make up some of this work." Confidentially, she added, "If you do not, I have no other choice but to flunk you for the entire quarter."

Marty hunched over in his seat, seemingly oblivious of everyone.

"Marty," said Mrs. Buell, more forcefully. "Don't you care?"

He stared up sullenly at her and ground his jaw. His eyes were shadowed, but they held a dark, cutting intensity. "Of course, I care," he uttered through clenched teeth.

Marty left immediately after class before I could speak to him. But I saw him at noon as I was entering the lunchroom with my tray and sack lunch. I was on my way to meet Becky when he hailed me over to his table. I could tell right away that his spirits had improved. "Hey, Tim!" he greeted. "How ya doing, man?"

"OK," I said, glancing over at Becky. She was sitting three tables away with her friends from the youth group.

Marty followed my gaze. "Hey, man, how are all your Bible buddies?"

"They're all right." I tried to sound casual and pretend nothing had happened. But all I could see in my mind was Marty being pushed into that squad car while all my new Christian friends watched in disgust. After a moment, I realized Marty was waiting for me to say something else, so I asked, "How are you doing?"

"OK," he replied noncommittally, then brightened. "Hey, man, why don't you sit down?"

I looked over at Becky and caught her eye. "Hey, Tim!" she called expectantly.

I gave Marty an apologetic half-smile. "I'd like to join you, man, but I promised Becky."

"Yeah, sure, you better get going," he muttered, waving me off.

As I passed Dennis's table, he motioned for me to join Traci and him. I laughed nervously and mumbled something about Becky waiting for me. "Maybe some other time, Tim?" asked Traci, sounding hopeful.

I nodded absently and sat down at last beside Becky. But for all my effort, she was busy now talking with her friend Jennie.

"Here," she said, handing Jennie a note. "Tell Jill to tell Bob to tell Steve that I'm not talking to Dave anymore, and he should call me if he wants to talk. Give this to Bob yourself and tell me what he says."

"Your phone number's on here!" exclaimed Jennie.

"So what?" said Becky lightly. After several other girls at the table greeted me, Becky whirled around in mock surprise and said, "Oh, hi, Tim. We were just talking about the, uh, retreat."

"Oh, yeah?"

"Yeah," she said, her voice as buoyant as a beach ball. "Ron asked me to be his canoe partner, but I said I'd really have to pray about it. And Larry asked me and I said maybe, and, uh, Frank asked me—" she rolled her eyes "—but we're not really on the same wavelength, if you know what I mean."

I forced a laugh, but she had lost me a mile ago.

"Well?" she coaxed, her blonde hair shimmering as she tilted her head just so.

I shrugged in bewilderment. "What?"

"Are you going to ask me, or not?"

Suddenly the light dawned. "Oh, I'm sorry. Yeah! Do you want to be my canoe partner?"

Becky gave me that sly, kittenish smile that said, *I thought you'd never ask!* "By the way, Tim," she rushed on brightly, "some of the kids from church are going to Mid-America this weekend. Do you want to go?"

I opened my lunch sack and took out a ham sandwich. "I don't know, Becky. I'm sort of short on cash at the moment, and actually, I'm not much for amusement parks."

"Oh, sure you are! Come on. It would be fun!"

"Well, all right," I said, bumbling. "Would you—I mean, can I take you?"

"Oh, really, Tim?" she fluttered, as if it were all my idea in the first place. "Of course, I'd love to go with you!" Her voice grew coy as she added, "Do you want me to wait and walk home from school with you this afternoon?"

"Naw. I usually take the bus," I replied. "Besides, tonight I've got to run an errand—gotta stop off at the pet store for some food for my tropical fish."

"Tropical fish?" Becky laughed, as if I'd just cracked the world's funniest joke. "Oh, Tim, how absolutely quaint you are!"

I wasn't sure whether she'd just handed me a compliment or an insult, and I wasn't about to ask.

When I stopped by the local pet store after school, I was surprised to see Traci working there. She was getting ready to lock up, but as soon as she spotted me, she came right over and said, "Hi, Tim. Can I help you?"

"Hi, Traci. I didn't know you worked here."

"Yeah. I love animals."

"Great. Me too. It's funny, but for a second I almost didn't recognize you—"

"Yeah, I know how it is," she smiled. "I kind of blend in with the animals, right?"

"No, that's not it," I protested. "It's just that we haven't had much chance to get acquainted."

"Sure, I know. Becky keeps you pretty busy."

"You noticed, huh?"

"Yeah, sort of." She shrugged questioningly. "So what can I do for you?"

"Oh, you mean, what'd I come here for?"

"Right. We've got a great sale on angora kittens—"

"No, thanks. I don't need any animals. You see, I've got this problem—"

"A problem?"

"Yeah, well, not me. It's my angel fish. They aren't reproducing."

"That's too bad."

"You got anything that'll help?"

"Uh-mm, angel fish? I think so. Just a minute." Traci stooped down behind the counter and examined several containers. Then she straightened up and handed me a small white box. "This ought to do it."

I read the label aloud. "Chopped horsefly mandibles, shrimp eggs, mosquito parts, tropical flies and other insects—" I pretended to gag. "They're gonna eat this stuff?"

"They'll fight for it," laughed Traci.

I opened the box and removed the plastic bag containing the fish food. "Hey, I'm not gonna get busted for having this stuff, am I?"

"Of course not. Why?"

"I kid you not, it looks just like marijuana!"

Traci shook her head. "Nobody will have a problem with it if they just smell it."

I took a whiff and laughed. "You're absolutely right. It's awful!"

73

Traci rang up the sale.

"How much do I owe you?" I asked.

"Four seventy-five."

"Wow, this is caviar, right?"

"I know. For that money you could feed them steak," she said with a sympathetic smile. Our gaze held for a moment. I hadn't noticed before what a gentle, sensitive face Traci had.

"Tim?" she asked tentatively. "Can I ask you something?"

"Yeah, Traci?"

"Would you like to come to our Bible study? I tried to tell you about it before, at the car wash."

I hedged. "Bible study?"

"Yeah. Dennis and I started it. Mrs. Buell is our sponsor—"

"At school?"

"Right. We could sure use a good leader—"

I quickly shook my head. "I'm really not the leader type, Traci." I thought right away of Marty and my dad. They were born leaders, but not me. Not by a long shot!

"I think you'd make a great leader, Tim," insisted Traci. Shyly she glanced down, tracing the wood grain on the counter. "To tell you the truth, Tim, you're the one who inspired this Bible study."

I stared at her, my mouth gaping in astonishment. "I don't understand—"

She gazed up at me, her eyes wide and sincere. "Remember that day you dropped your Bible on the bus?"

I felt my face grow warm. "That's right. You were sitting across from me. I'm sorry. I guess I was kind of uptight—"

"No, no," corrected Traci. "That was really something. I mean, you weren't afraid to bring your Bible to school. That's what inspired me to start our Bible study."

"For real?" I was having a hard time finding the right words.

"Yeah. I figured there was somebody else around school who wasn't ashamed of the Lord. It kinda encouraged me."

"Me? Wow! I never thought I encouraged anybody!" I hesitated as some of my euphoria evaporated. "I don't even bring my Bible to school anymore."

"You could always start again. You could bring it to our Bible study."

I nodded thoughtfully. "Yeah, I—I just might do that."

10

On Saturday I took Becky to Mid-America, the most popular amusement park in our part of the state. Only trouble is, it costs a bundle too, and Becky wasn't satisfied to go on just a few rides. She was like a kid turned loose in a candy store, running from the roller coaster to the Ferris wheel, from the cotton candy stand to the fast food concession area. I could hardly keep up with her. And all the time, she was giggling and screaming non-stop!

We rode every ride in the place at least twice, even the merry-go-round, and we pigged out on hot dogs, ice cream bars, and popcorn until I thought I was going to barf. But that still wasn't enough for Becky.

She dragged me over to the shooting galleries and arcade games, wheedling, "Please, Tim, win me a teddy bear. Come on, you can do it. I know you can!"

Relentingly I forked over the rest of my cash and made a fool of myself trying to shoot down painted ducks, knock over milk bottles, and toss rings around bowling pins. Finally, after half a dozen games of Speed Ball, I managed to win a stuffed giant orange bear. It was bigger than both of us and ugly as could be, with its googly eyes and red felt tongue.

Becky shrieked with rapture.

As we left the arcade area—with me carrying the bear, naturally—Becky brushed back her hair and said breathlessly, "Oh, I'm so dizzy!"

"From all the rides?" I asked.

She hugged my arm and laughed. "No, from you, silly!"

I smiled, too tired to be flattered, and said, "Hey, are you about ready to go home?"

"Are you kidding?" she cried. "I wanna go on at least two more roller coaster rides!"

"We're all out of money." I turned my pocket inside out for emphasis.

"Oh, but Tim," she gushed. "It was worth it!" She tweaked the bear's button nose. "He's so cute!"

We made our way through the crush of the crowds, away from the Day-glo banners and streams of fluorescent lights, over to a private, shaded area. "Becky," I began haltingly, "there was something I really wanted to talk to you about."

She gave me a curious glance. "OK. We could sit down here on the bench."

I nodded and sat down. She sat down beside me, closer than I expected. "What is it, Tim?" she asked softly.

I shifted nervously, wishing I had a little more room. "Well, it's something I've been wanting to talk to you about for a while, but it's kind of hard to say."

Becky looked me straight in the eyes and murmured warmly, "Go on, Tim. I'm ready."

I struggled for just the right words. This was something I'd been thinking about ever since I talked with Traci at the pet store.

"Becky," I declared, summoning my courage, "I

really feel like I've let the Lord down."

She stared at me in amazement, then burst into laughter. "Oh, Tim," she exclaimed, her voice edged with irritation, "is that all you're worried about?"

"Well, yeah, I mean—"

"Tim Hughes," she scolded teasingly, "you've been spinning around too much today!"

"Seriously, Becky," I persisted, "haven't you ever wondered what it would be like if we really started to live for the Lord at Roosevelt?"

"We'd get slaughtered," she said dryly.

Now that I'd gone this far, I wasn't about to give up. "Picture it, Becky," I urged. "Us Christians bringing Jesus' love right into our school. Caring about hurting kids—kids that are failing, kids with problems at home. Can you imagine it?"

"Sure. I see a big pile of beat-up, unpopular Christian kids."

I guess she could see I didn't like her answer, because she softened and said, "Look, Tim. If you want to be a Christian at Roosevelt, be a Christian. But keep your mouth shut about it."

I looked away and scowled. "We've been keeping our mouth shut long enough, Becky. If kids use God's name as a curse word, if a teacher cuts down the Lord during a lecture on evolution—it's time we stood up for the Lord—and lived for Him too."

Becky was about to interrupt, but I was on a roll now, saying all the things that had been building up in me for weeks. "Roosevelt needs to see God's love in action, Becky. We've got to get out of our clique and start reaching out to the lonely kids on the fringes. How are they going to know about Jesus if we don't tell them?"

"Just what do you suggest, Tim?" she asked thickly.

"Well, for starters, how about if we go to Traci's Bible study? I hear there are a lot of kids in her group who—"

"—who are retarded!" finished Becky sharply.

We had reached an impasse. We stared darkly at each other, neither of us saying a word. Finally Becky stood up, gathered the giant bear in her arms, and announced, "You're right, Tim. It's time to go home!"

A few days later, I realized that my resolve to stand up for the Lord was just beginning to be tested. I arrived home from school to an empty house. I knew Dad was probably working late at the studio, but usually Mom was home, fixing something good for dinner or typing away on her romance novel. But today the house seemed even larger than usual, ringing with a hollow silence.

I glanced around the living room and noticed the mail sitting untouched on the coffee table. I flipped through the bills and ads, then stared in disbelief at several books I hadn't seen before—*Understanding the Occult*, *How to Deprogram Your Child from Christianity*, and a hefty volume on teenage rebellion.

I slammed the books down in disgust, then noticed the note on the TV. It said, "Honey, your dad and I have gone to Roosevelt to see Mrs. Buell. Be back at 5:30. Love, Mom."

"Now what's that all about?" I wondered aloud as I headed for the kitchen. I loaded myself down with potato chips, onion dip, two bananas, a box of cookies, and a carton of orange juice, then returned to the living room. I made myself comfortable on the sofa, picked up the remote control and flipped through the television channels. My dad's talk show was on. Dad sat there on his "throne" interviewing a sullen-looking Moslem youth. "As a terrorist," said Dad in his usual polished tones, "how do you feel after you've killed someone?"

"What do you mean—feel?" grunted the scowling terrorist. "We cannot feel!"

I quickly switched the channel to a cartoon I used to watch as a kid. I settled back and reached for the chips. Maybe for just a little while I could forget my problems. But within a few minutes my curiosity got the best of me. I had to find out what Mom and Dad were seeing Mrs. Buell about.

I got on my ten-speed and biked back to Roosevelt High. I stood outside Mrs. Buell's partially open door, debating whether to knock or just go in. I could see my folks standing beside Mrs. Buell's desk. A couple of guys—rowdies in sunglasses and heavy-metal tee shirts—sat at the back of the room doing makeup work.

I hesitated as I heard Mrs. Buell say, "Tim has a B + average, and he always turns in his work on time—"

Dad leaned forward confidentially and said, "Mrs. Buell, we wanted to talk to you about something else."

"Yes?"

"Well," continued Dad uneasily, "Tim went up to this Christian camp last summer, and—well, he had one of those 'conversion experiences.' "

"He got, uh, born again," explained Mom.

Now I knew I couldn't just barge in on their conversation!

"Born again?" echoed Mrs. Buell. "I see."

"Yeah," said Dad gravely, "and we think Tim might be in a cult—"

"He's not in a cult, dear," corrected Mom.

Dad frowned. "Well, we're—worried."

"We're not worried," contradicted Mom. "We're hoping he's in remission, if you know what I mean." Her voice broke with emotion. "Tim was such an all-American boy."

"He used to party, go after the girls," Dad reminisced. "Just like I did when I was a kid."

Mom glared at Dad, so he changed the subject fast. "Uh, Mrs. Buell, Tim wants to be a missionary now, and he knows there's no money in it."

"They would pay him something," argued Mom.

One of the detainees sauntered up to the desk to turn in his paper. Dad was too busy ranting on to notice him. "Tim buys Christian records with his allowance money," Dad exclaimed. "And we've even caught him in bed—" spotting the rowdy listening with leering interest, Dad emphasized sarcastically "—reading religious literature!"

"The Bible, Sidney."

Dad ignored Mom. "Now, Mrs. Buell, can you tell me that this is normal behavior for a sixteen-year-old?"

"He's seventeen now, dear."

"All right, seventeen!" Dad was disgruntled now.

Mrs. Buell smiled patiently. "Mr. and Mrs. Hughes, please hold on a minute," she urged. "Let me tell you that there are a number of so-called Christians here at Roosevelt High, and most of them don't do anything but talk."

Mom and Dad looked temporarily consoled.

But I'd heard enough. I couldn't believe my parents had dumped all their warped ideas and suspicions on poor, unsuspecting Mrs. Buell. I turned and stalked off down the hall, then pedaled home with a burst of speed, propelled by mushrooming anger and resentment.

The mood at the dinner table that evening was dismal at best. We ate in stony silence—until Dad hit on a new tactic.

"Why don't you give some of your soccer friends a call?" he suggested with a studied casualness. Man, I could see through his motives right away.

"They drink too much," I muttered.

Mom, her voice dripping with sweetness, came back with, "What would be wrong with calling some of your old friends from your Scout patrol?"

I rolled my eyes in exasperation. "They're not my type anymore, Mom. All they do is play video games."

"Well, what about Alex Rundel?" persisted Dad.

"He ran away from home."

"OK, what about that Dave fellow?"

"Dave Little? Drug overdose. St. Mary's."

"Well, what ever happened to the guy who came around here on the weekends and ate like a horse—Larry, uh—"

"Reed?"

"Yeah."

"Department of Corrections." I shook my head in frustration. "Look, Dad, why can't I just hang around with the kids I want to?"

"You mean, from the church!" exclaimed Dad, aggravated.

"Sure, why not from the church?" I sat back in my chair and rubbed my hand over my face. I didn't want to argue with Dad like this. I was losing control, and I knew it. "OK, Dad, do you want me to go out drinking and partying again? Is that what you want?"

I noticed Dad clenching and unclenching his fist

with a nervous irritation. "No, not just drinking, but—"

My voice was ragged now. I was riding my emotions; the words came spilling out. "Well, that's what's going to happen, and you don't care, do you?"

"I think we're making a lot of fuss over a few beers—"

"And reefers, and pills?"

"You don't have to do everything they do," raged Dad.

My voice grew shrill. "But you don't mind if I end up like them, do you!" I shoved back my chair and stood up. The chair toppled over behind me. "Do you!" For the first time in my life I was shouting back at my dad.

Mom broke in helplessly with, "Sid, this isn't what you want!"

"What I want is for this kid to show some normal social behavior!" roared Dad. He caught the pained expression in Mom's eyes and retreated a little. "Look, Tim," he said, struggling to regain his composure, "I'd just like to see you—like regular guys, that's all."

I tossed my napkin on my plate and retorted miserably, "All right, Dad, I'll do what you want. See if it makes you feel any better!"

As I stalked out of the room, I heard Mom shout at Dad, "You really blew it this time, Sidney Hughes!"

11

I had a hard time sleeping that night. I knew I had really blown it with my dad, and now I felt a heavy mixture of frustration and guilt. It seemed that there was friction in all my relationships—with my parents, with Marty, even with Becky. If Jesus had come to bring peace, how come my life was in such turmoil?

As I tossed and turned, I thought about what Mrs. Buell had said about most Christian kids being just a lot of talk. Was that true?

Did Jesus make a difference in my life? Did I want Him to?

I remembered what Becky had told me at the amusement park: *Be a Christian if you want to, Tim, but keep your mouth shut about it.* Was that how I wanted to live?

Then I recalled Traci at the pet store and the sincere expression in her eyes when she told me I had inspired her to start the Bible study at school. Me, Tim Hughes—the guy who could stand in the middle of a room and be invisible! I had made a difference. I had influenced someone to take a stand for Jesus. And it was such a simple, little thing I had done—carrying my Bible to school. But it had encouraged someone else to do something for Jesus too.

Maybe that was what it was all about—starting somewhere and doing something for Jesus, even if you figured it didn't amount to much and wouldn't make a difference.

Finally, I slipped out of bed and got down on my knees in the dark and choked out a prayer. "Jesus, I'm not a high-powered, leader-type guy like my dad or even like Marty. But I know You love me, and I'd sure like to let other people know You love them too. I don't want to keep my mouth shut like Becky says, or be just a lot of idle talk like Mrs. Buell says." My face felt wet. I couldn't keep back the tears. "I want to show people Your love, especially Marty and my folks. I guess You already know I'm not much for taking a stand. Lord, I sure do need You."

The next day, I attended Traci's Bible study. Six guys and gals were there. Mrs. Buell sat at her desk grading papers. She looked up and smiled when I entered the room.

Traci looked pretty pleased too. "Tim, I'm so glad you came."

"Hey, Tim!" greeted Dennis and the others.

I sat down beside Traci and asked, "What's happening?"

"We're trying to decide how to reach the kids in our school and the people in our community for Jesus. Do you have any ideas?"

I shrugged. "It's not going to happen overnight, but I think we've got to start meeting some of their needs."

"He's right," said one of the girls. "We should try to reach people that no one really cares about."

"People with problems," said Dennis.

"So how do we go about finding these people?"

questioned a guy named Larry.

"They're everywhere—" I said.

"The dregs of society?" scoffed Larry. "Come on, you think it's necessary—?"

I nodded. "How are people going to know the love of Jesus if we don't show it to them?"

"That's the whole point of us going out, Larry," said Traci.

"If we don't reach out to these people, then who will?"

"You can't do it without a plan. You got a plan, Tim?"

"Yeah. Yeah, sure. Maybe I do. We could start by playing basketball with some inner city kids and visiting a few nursing homes in the area."

"And we could tutor kids in danger of failing," suggested Traci.

"Right!" I agreed. "I think we can come up with a lot of ways to help others."

During the next couple of weeks, our Bible study group was busy with all sorts of activities. We did odd jobs for our neighbors, took groceries to some welfare families, and visited some shut-ins. We taught some youngsters how to swim and ride a bike and took a new puppy to a little boy whose dog had been hit by a car. I even tried a little tutoring, although I must admit that turned out to be a rather ticklish situation.

Bonnie was a good-looking blonde who had other things in mind than being tutored. While I was quizzing her on history dates, she figured we should be making a little history of our own. "Don't I turn you on?" she cooed as she cuddled up to me.

I shifted uncomfortably. "Yeah, I mean, you're not bad looking."

"So where are we going after this?"

"Nowhere. We have to study."

"I am studying," she said dreamily, her face just inches from mine.

"I, uh, mean the textbook, not me."

"Usually when I go on my dates, we get right to the point," she said cozily.

"We're doing history dates," I reminded her.

"You mean, you really came over here just to tutor me?"

"Yeah, that's the idea."

She sat back and gave me a baffled smile. "Tim Hughes, somehow you're different, you know? I like that."

I finished tutoring Bonnie around ten and arrived home just as my dad was pulling into the driveway. Mom had already gone to bed, so we both stole quietly to the kitchen to raid the refrigerator. Dad fixed himself a bologna sandwich; I opened a can of chili.

"I guess your mother had to eat alone tonight," said Dad, sitting down at the table.

I poured my chili into a saucepan. "She probably didn't mind. This morning she said she was going to spend all day on her book."

"Yeah, that silly romance novel," scoffed Dad. "I think your mother has visions of someday writing the Great American Novel."

"So what's wrong with that, Dad? Why don't you let her dream?"

"Who's stopping her?"

"Well, you don't support her or encourage her."

"Why should I? It's all a lot of mush and fluff nonsense!"

I looked sharply at Dad. "See, you put her down just

like you put me down for wanting to be a missionary."

"Because they're both outrageous ideas."

"Why, Dad? Because they're not your idea of what we should do?"

Dad bit into his sandwich as if he hadn't heard me.

I sat down across from him with my bowl of chili. "Did your dad want you to be a talk show host?"

He scowled. "No, he certainly didn't."

"What'd he want you to be?"

A strange flicker of memory crossed Dad's face. He blinked several times and looked away. "My father was a very strong man, Tim, a perfectionist, very authoritative. I never saw him show any emotion except anger. And, frankly, I don't think I could have pleased him even if I'd been President of the United States."

I stared down into my chili. Dad had never talked about Grandpa Hughes before. I felt a little awkward, as if I'd glimpsed something Dad hadn't intended for me to see. "He died when I was about four, didn't he?" I asked.

"Four or five. I'm lousy with dates."

"It's been so long," I remarked quietly. "I guess you don't think about him much anymore."

Dad gave me a long, cryptic stare. "He's never out of my mind for a minute, Tim." He made a sound, half cough, half chuckle. "You know, it's funny. Sometimes I feel like he's actually walking around inside my skin."

I fiddled uneasily with my soup spoon. "I guess you're a lot like him, huh?"

Dad's eyebrows arched in surprise. "You think so? I vowed I'd never be like him." It must have finally occurred to Dad that he was saying too much, because his expression suddenly closed up tight, and I couldn't read any more emotion in his face. He was his usual self again. "So how was your day, Tim?" he asked in his buoyant voice.

I felt let down inside, like for a minute I'd seen through a crack in Dad's armor and found a person who was as vulnerable as I was, and now he'd sealed off the crack and maybe I'd never see inside again.

"I guess we've both had a pretty long day," Dad mused when I didn't reply.

"Yeah, a long day," I said quickly. "Good, though. Busy."

"School and all that?"

"Yeah. I ran some errands for Mrs. Kelso down the street. She broke her leg, you know."

"Oh, right. I heard about that." He paused and gave me a sly smile. "I suppose you were out on some hot date tonight."

"No, I was tutoring a girl from school. She'll flunk history if she doesn't pass the mid-term."

Dad studied me curiously. "You know, I went golfing with Howard Noland the other day. He said you and your church group brought over a new puppy for his son, Tommy. Howard was quite impressed by your gesture of good will."

I rubbed my arm self-consciously. "Tommy's dog got run over by a car. We just wanted to make him feel better."

One corner of Dad's mouth curled slightly. "You're becoming quite the Good Samaritan lately, aren't you?"

I shrugged. My heart started pounding. "I'm just trying to—to show people Jesus' love, Dad," I murmured.

Saying those words was one of the hardest things I'd ever done, but I sure felt good inside after I'd said them.

Dad finished his sandwich in silence. I wondered if by mentioning Jesus' name I'd violated some unspoken rule between us. I broke the silence with a stab at casual conversation. "So how was your day, Dad?"

He grimaced. "It was a bear."

"Really tough, huh?"

"Incredible, Tim. Totally off the wall." I could tell that Dad was warming to the subject. "I think my guests are getting crazier every day," he said with a hint of amusement. "Today I interviewed a professor who specializes in computer technology. He claims that computers are going to take over the entire world in four and a half years. Another guy identified himself only as Mr. X. He stayed in the shadows with a hood over his head, and I still don't have the foggiest idea what he was talking about."

"It sounds—interesting," I murmured.

Dad shook his head wearily. "You know, Tim, sometimes I wonder what it's all about—"

His words hung in the air between us for a full minute before I replied, "Yeah, I used to wonder that too, Dad."

"But not anymore?"

I made myself look him straight in the eye as I said, "I don't have to wonder anymore."

Dad changed the subject. "So, is this the weekend you'll be taking the canoe trip with that church crowd?"

"No, Dad, that's the following weekend. This weekend I'm going to a Cubs game at Wrigley Field."

"Hey, I haven't been to a baseball game in years!"

"Why don't you come with us, Dad?"

"Us?" Dad's eyes clouded. "Don't tell me. You're going with your youth group."

"Well, yeah. Steve, the leader, asked me, but you're welcome to come—"

Dad stood up and unbuttoned his shirt. "Listen, kiddo, I almost forgot. I promised Howard Noland a rematch this Saturday at the country club. I beat the socks off him! He wouldn't pack up his clubs until I agreed on another go-round." Dad cuffed my shoulder good-naturedly. "You know, Tim, in the six years Noland and I have played golf together, he's never beat me. Would you believe it?"

I straightened my shoulders reflexively and nodded. "Yeah, Dad. I believe it."

12

I had a great time at the Cubs game with Steve and the guys on Saturday. The Cubs played the New York Mets and won 9 - 8, with extra innings. The tension in the air was awesome. In fact, I cheered so loud I got hoarse.

Afterward, I caught a ride home with Steve. I had a lot of things on my mind, so I was glad we could talk privately. He drove to the beach, and we walked along the water's edge just as the sun was setting. After the crowds and heat and noise of the stadium, that cool sand and brisk breeze felt fantastic.

Steve has a way of making a guy think without putting him down and a natural way of talking about the Lord that makes you feel comfortable. "You're a real Cubs fan, aren't you, Tim?" he asked conversationally.

"I sure am. Win or lose, I'm loyal."

"No one would doubt that—the way you cheered them on. I'm surprised you still have any voice left."

I smiled, pleased. I was still riding high with energy and excitement, and I wanted to put it into words. "Man, that game was all right! You know, Steve, it feels good to get so involved, to care so much about the team that you just want to shout and cheer and tell the whole world how you feel."

Steve nodded. "That's sort of what it means to be a fan of Jesus Christ."

I looked at him. "Fan? You mean 'Christian,' don't you?"

"Same difference," said Steve.

I stared down at the sand. "Yeah, I think I see what you mean." Suddenly, all the questions and frustrations I'd been feeling lately crowded my mind. "I've been wondering, Steve—"

"What's that, Tim?"

The words didn't come easy. "I wonder if I've been as, uh, loyal to Jesus Christ as I've been to the Cubs team?"

"Only you can answer that, Tim."

"I've been trying, but I'm really confused about something."

"Do you want to tell me about it?" said Steve.

I kicked absently at a stone. "My best friend Marty— the guy who tried to steal the carwash money—he needs to hear about Christ, but I haven't told him."

"Any reason why not?"

"Well, the Bible says we're not supposed to hang around with kids who smoke dope and drink and stuff like that, so I've been avoiding him."

"I can appreciate your dilemma, Tim," replied Steve.

"So what do I do about it?"

"The Bible calls Christians to be clean and pure and separate. But that doesn't mean living in an isolation chamber. We're supposed to get the world out of ourselves, but not ourselves out of the world."

I shrugged, puzzled. "That sounds like double talk to me."

Steve pulled a small New Testament from his shirt pocket and thumbed through it. There wasn't much light left, so he had to strain to read. "Here's how Jesus handled that problem, Tim. He was talking about the Pharisees and teachers of the law who complained to his disciples, 'Why do you eat and drink with tax collectors and sinners?' Jesus answered them, 'It is not the healthy who need a doctor, but the sick. I have not come to call the righteous, but sinners to repentance.'"

I shook my head in amazement. "Here I thought it was my duty to avoid people like Marty, but Jesus made it a point to go out and find people like him!"

"Because Jesus loved them and had the good news of salvation to share with them, Tim."

I stared out at the horizon. The sun looked like a fat, ripe orange that I could just reach out and pluck. I could imagine it solid in my hand, and in my mouth, sweet and juicy. Even as I watched, it was suddenly gone, lost in shadows.

"You still have questions, don't you, Tim?" said Steve with a knowing glance.

I met his gaze. "Yeah, I do," I admitted. "There's one more thing that bothers me."

"I'm listening."

"Well, Jesus is God, and He didn't have to worry all the time about being tempted to do something wrong. I mean, how do I know I won't end up going Marty's way instead of getting him to come mine?"

Steve chuckled lightly. "You really do know how to get right to the essentials, don't you, Tim?"

"I just want to know what Jesus expects of me."

Steve gripped my shoulder reassuringly. "First of all, you might be surprised to know that Jesus was tempted in every possible way that we're tempted today."

I stared at him in astonishment. "You mean—everything?"

"In every way that a person can be tempted. I mean, the devil even put in a personal appearance."

"Yeah, but wasn't it just a formality? I mean, God can't sin."

"Don't forget, Tim. Jesus was every bit as much a man as He was God. He experienced every temptation as any man would, but He resisted every temptation as only God could."

"That's just it," I exclaimed. "I'm not God! How do I know I'll do the right thing and resist temptations?" I hesitated, remembering something. "The other night, there was this girl, and I mean, she was coming on to me—"

"And you were tempted?"

I felt my face grow warm. "Well, yeah. She wasn't my type, but—you know—"

"You resisted?"

I nodded.

"How?"

"I don't know. I just knew it wasn't right. It was like Jesus was right there with me, and I didn't want to let Him down."

"What you were experiencing, Tim, was the Holy Spirit within you," explained Steve. "You were right when you said you aren't God, but as a Christian, God does dwell within you in the form of His Holy Spirit. So, in that sense, you're equipped to face temptations just as Jesus was."

"Wow! I never thought of it like that." I looked directly at Steve. "What you're saying is, I can reach out to Marty because Jesus is reaching out to him too!"

"He's reaching out *through you*," said Steve. "Go

for it, Tim! I'll be praying for you both.''

When I arrived home that night, I was really excited over the idea of healing the breech between Marty and me. I cared about Marty, and now I knew it was all right to care. In fact, Jesus wanted me to show Marty *His* love.

But I didn't expect to have that chance the very next day. After church on Sunday morning, a bunch of us stayed to make plans for the canoe trip the following weekend. After our meeting, I happened to pass through the empty sanctuary, and there, sitting alone in a front pew, was Marty, his head bowed, his shoulders slumped. Shafts of light filtered through the stained glass window, casting a fragmented glow over his rusty hair and solemn, irregular features. I watched him, stunned. What was he doing here?

After a minute he pulled himself to his feet and walked hesitantly up to the altar. He gazed down at a large, open Bible, his expression twisted, tormented. I was about to go to him, when several members of the youth group burst into the sanctuary, laughing and gossiping about who was going to be whose canoe partner on the retreat. I was sure they saw Marty, but they ignored him, walking on and chatting among themselves without even a curious backward glance.

"Hey, Sherry, you gonna be my partner?''

"Maybe, if you ask real nice.''

"Know what I heard? Cindy is going on the canoe trip with John!''

"You're kidding!''

As they left the sanctuary without a word to Marty, I noticed a contemptuous sneer harden on his face. He shoved the Bible away, pivoted sharply and strode out of the church, the sound of his steps echoing hollowly in the empty sanctuary.

I stole up to the altar and glanced at the Scripture Marty had been reading. The Bible was open to John 15. My eyes fell on verse 13: "Greater love hath no man than this, that a man lay down his life for his friends."

I pivoted and ran down the aisle to the vestibule after Marty. He had already gone out the door and was taking the steps two at a time. I shoved open the door and darted out. "Marty, wait!"

He whirled around and stared at me. "Where'd you come from?"

"I was inside. You didn't see me."

"Yeah, but I saw your Bible buddies. They pretended they didn't see me."

"I know." We walked along the sidewalk toward the parking lot. "Where's your car?" I asked, hooking my thumbs on my jeans.

"What do you care?"

"I got my dad's wheels if you need a ride."

"Naw. It's a nice day to walk."

I was batting zero, so I tried another tactic. "Marty, I was wondering if you wanted any help."

"Help?"

"Yeah. To catch up on your work. I—I heard you got kicked out of school."

Marty jumped on the defensive. "Hey, I didn't get kicked out of school, all right? I decided to leave."

"OK, OK. I just wanted to know if I could help out."

"What, so you'd tutor me then? You'd get your Christian Brownie points for the day? Sorry!"

I gripped Marty's arm, then stared in disbelief at his bandaged wrist. "Hey, Marty, what happened, man?"

He jerked his hand away.

"What did you do, man?" I asked softly.

Marty wouldn't meet my gaze. The tendons in his neck tightened. He ran his hand through the mop of red hair on his forehead. "Look, Tim," he said finally, his eyes flashing fire, "you think I've got it all together, but I don't, all right? My parents are getting divorced, I'm flunking out of school, and I've lost my best friend."

All I could manage was, "I'm sorry, man."

"Yeah," he said darkly, lifting his bandaged wrist. "I always wanted to see what it was like to give to the blood bank. But I made a mess of that, too."

"Marty, listen—"

Sarcastically, he added, "And I ain't been down to Mexico picking up cocaine. I've been in a drug rehabilitation center at River Oaks."

"I never knew," I uttered.

Marty was going strong now, spilling out all his pent-up feelings. "Look, Tim. Ever since first grade, me and you have been best friends. Then, suddenly, you become a Christian and you don't want to get contaminated anymore. What have I done that you have to avoid me, man? I'm walking down the hall in school, and you pretend not to see me. I call up on the phone, and you're not home—but I hear you in the background. What's with you, Tim?"

Marty's bitterness and pain stung me worse than a slap in the face. There was so much I wanted to say, but it all came down to one fact. "I was ashamed, Marty. Forgive me?"

He scowled and looked away.

"Listen, Marty," I urged, touching his arm. "Why don't you come to church with me tonight?"

"Church, man!" he scoffed. "I just been in church, and what good did it do me?" He stalked off with a curt, "So long, Tim. I've got to go check out a motor-cycle."

13

I really felt miserable as I drove home from church that morning. Here I had finally determined to patch things up with Marty, and he had turned me down cold. How was I going to show him Jesus' love if he wouldn't even talk to me?

Now that I had blown it with Marty, I figured the day was all downhill from here on out. I was right.

I knew the minute I stepped inside my front door that my parents were having a real intense conversation in the living room, and I'd better not interrupt. I stood quietly in the hallway, out of sight, waiting for a chance to sneak through to my room. Then I realized with a start that they were talking about me!

Mom was saying, "Sid, I've been very concerned about Timmy lately."

"Yeah, me too," said Dad.

"It's those new friends he hangs around with."

"Here it comes," Dad muttered. "OK, Meg, what is it?"

"Well, I was uptown the other day, and I saw some of them. And they were very strange looking."

"Couldn't be any different than when we were kids, so what's the big deal?"

Mom's tone grew serious. "Sid, I was in Timmy's room today, and I found a whole bag of marijuana on top of his desk."

"Pot? Really?"

"Sid, aren't you upset?"

"Well, I'm surprised, yeah. Concerned."

"This isn't like Tim. Even before camp."

"It's not the end of the world, Meg. It's probably a passing phase. A lot of kids his age occasionally take recreational drugs."

"Recreational drugs!"

"Come on, Meg. The way you sound, it's my fault he's taking the stuff."

"Well, you are the one who told him to start loosening up!"

"Fine! Let him grow up to be a missionary in some cockamamie jungle!"

I couldn't take any more. I walked into the room and stared hard at Mom and Dad. For a long minute no one said anything. I felt a lump in my throat as big as a golf ball. I sat down on the couch across from them. Finally, I found my voice. "Mom, Dad, I couldn't help but hear your conversation."

Mom looked sheepish. "We thought you were still at church, Timmy."

"I know. I didn't drive Becky today, so I came right home." I looked at Mom. "You don't have to worry about me. That was fish food you found today in my room. And those weird kids are dropouts our school Bible study group is trying to help out."

"Oh, Timmy—"

I went over and gave Mom a hug, then glanced at Dad. "Dad—?"

He looked away.

I reached over and touched his shoulder. "Dad, I've tried so hard to please you." My voice was gravelly with emotion. "I don't know what else to do. But I—I love you both very much."

After I had tried to smooth things out with Mom and Dad, I decided to try again with Marty. He had said this morning that he wouldn't come to church with me. But maybe there was still a way to convince him.

I wasn't sure what my plan would be until later that afternoon when I picked up Becky for the evening youth program. She could tell that I was deep in thought. Inching over closer, she asked softly, "What are you thinking about?"

"I don't know," I murmured distractedly.

"It must be something important," she purred. "Is it me?"

"Actually, I was just thinking about Marty," I admitted. "What if he became a Christian?"

Becky sounded disappointed. "Yeah, we'll really have to pray for him."

"I have been."

Becky sighed dramatically. "I have such a burden for him."

"You know, I was thinking something else," I said carefully. "We're in his neighborhood."

"Oh, Tim," she scoffed, "he's not dangerous. He's not going to pull anything on us."

"Hey, I know that. But why don't we stop by his house and see if he wants to go to church with us?" I suggested, as if the idea had just occurred to me.

"What?" She laughed nervously. "I'm glad you're only joking!"

"I'm not."

"Tim, he's not going to fit!"

"Sure, he will."

Becky folded her arms in exasperation. "I don't see why you're trying to do this to someone who's so against the Lord." She glanced at me, her mouth settling into a perturbed pout. "I really wanted to be alone with you this afternoon, Tim."

"We'll be alone," I assured her with a grin. "You, me, and Marty!"

Becky was still pouting minutes later when I pulled into Marty's driveway. I left her in the car while I walked up to Marty's door and knocked.

Marty took his time answering, and when he did, I could tell by his expression that he was into something pretty heavy. I glanced past him into the kitchen. The bandage from his gouged wrist was on the table beside a mean-looking butcher knife. My stomach coiled in revolt. *Suicide!* He was playing with the idea again! I knew I couldn't leave Marty alone. Somehow I had to get him out of the house—now! I gave him a searching glance, but he looked away.

"What have you been doing, Marty?" I probed.

He stepped out of the doorway onto the porch and quickly shut the door behind him. "What are *you* doing here, Tim?" he said under his breath.

I forced my voice to remain calm. "Just figured I'd try again, Marty."

He glanced over at Becky. "What's she doing in the car?"

"We're going to church. I was hoping you would come with us."

"We covered that ground this morning, Tim."

"Yeah, I know, but I thought maybe you'd change your mind."

"Not a chance. Besides, I got plans with Debbie."

That was a stall, and I knew it. There was no way I was going to leave Marty alone. I'd stay and wrestle him to the ground if I had to, to keep him from taking his life. But Marty was nobody's fool. He would run hard and fast from anything that smacked of sympathy. Yet, if he stayed home, he would just sit and brood and—the possibility was unthinkable! If only I could get him to church where he could hear about Jesus—the only One who could really help him with his problems!

Idly, I picked up a basketball lying in the driveway, tried a lay-up shot, and missed.

"Man, you ain't so good at that," chuckled Marty. It was the first time I'd seen him smile in weeks.

An idea started brewing. "Hey, Marty, I'll tell you what. I'll play you for it! I win, you gotta come to church with us."

Marty eyed me with suspicion.

"And if you win," I continued, "I'll wash and wax your car for two months."

Marty snickered and took a drag on his cigarette. "Seems like a pretty easy way for me to get some free car washes."

I twirled the ball in anticipation, but I could see Becky sighing with exasperation. "Come on, you guys!" she called. "You're wasting time!"

"You serious about playing?" said Marty.

"Yep. Let's play till five."

I sank a basket, then Marty made two.

Becky was boiling. "We're going to be late for church!"

It was a close game, but I finally edged out Marty and won the bet. Grudgingly he climbed into the back seat and scrunched down, folding his arms across his chest. "Man, I can't believe this," he muttered.

You can't!" said Becky under her breath.

"I'm sure glad you could come with us, Marty," I said as I backed out into the street.

"Hey, Tim, I was supposed to meet Debbie, you know."

"Great. We'll pick her up on our way."

"No way, man. She ain't ever seen the inside of a church."

"She'll love it, man."

Debbie—a bleached blonde with gobs of makeup and a nasal twang—was waiting for Marty just as he said. In her tight tank top and slinky skirt, she looked like she was ready for anything but church. "Get in, Debbie," I told her as Marty opened the rear door. "You know Becky, don't you?"

"Hey, Beck! How's it going?" Debbie drawled as she snuggled close to Marty.

Becky spoke through clenched teeth. "Fine, thanks."

"Hey, Tim, turn up the tunes," said Marty.

Debbie sounded strung out. "Where we going, man?"

"We're going to a meeting," I told her.

"A church meeting," said Marty.

"Hey, man, get me out of here!"

Becky looked daggers at me. "If she doesn't want to go—"

"Be cool, Deb, all right?" urged Marty. "It's only an hour, and then we'll go party afterwards."

"Yeah, we'll go party," I joined in. "We'll hit the ice cream shop!"

"Uh—I feel like going home," said Becky darkly.

"Listen, man," said Debbie. "I heard there's gonna be a party at some guy's beach house tonight."

"We've already made plans, thanks," replied Becky in her loftiest tone.

Debbie wasn't about to give up. "Well, there's gonna be about a hundred and fifty people there. It's gonna be majorly big. It's gonna be open. It's gonna be massive kegs!"

I figured I'd better change the subject fast. "We got a little time before church. What d'ya say we pick up somebody else?"

"Now who?" declared Becky, dripping venom.

I took an abrupt turn and headed for Dennis's house. He was more than pleased to catch a ride with us. With a huge grin, he piled into the back seat between Debbie and Marty.

Becky gave me a withering glance. "I am really tired of all this, Tim!"

Debbie leaned forward and whispered sympathetically, "Don't sweat it, hon. If you're tired, ain't no reason you can't sleep in church."

I had no idea how angry Becky was with me until we headed for the ice cream shop after church. Marty and Debbie split right after the service, and Dennis rode home with Steve, so it was just the two of us at last. I figured Becky'd be pleased that we finally had a little time alone, but she was seething inside, ready to erupt.

"It was just a big mess," she complained. "They shouldn't have come. Do you think you're going to save the whole school or something? Do you know what kind of reputation you're going to get if you keep this up?"

"No, but I'm sure you'll tell me," I said quietly.

FIr⁻ ⁻A
GOSHEN, INDIANA 46526

I parked in front of the ice cream shop and we went inside. The rest of the youth group was already there, seated, devouring their ice cream and probably some juicy gossip as well.

"Tim, get me two scoops of rocky road," said Becky coolly.

I stood in line while she sat down at a table between Bill and Ron. I noticed that there weren't any empty seats. While I waited for our order, I could hear her high, bubbly laugh.

When I finally brought Becky her cone, she was totally engrossed in conversation with good old Willie McAllister the Third. She looked over momentarily and took her cone, then gestured breezily toward an empty table. "Have a seat, Tim."

I sat down with reluctance, aware that all the guys were watching curiously, no doubt wondering whether Becky was dumping me. Frankly, I wondered the same thing myself.

I didn't have to wonder long.

Becky turned to me, tilting her head and swinging her hair coyly. "Uh, say, Tim, you don't mind if I go driving around with these guys, do you?"

Startled, I asked, "Are you sure?"

"Yeah, I'll get a ride home. You don't need to worry."

Bill McAllister gave Ron a private smirk and quipped, loudly enough for me to hear, "He can always look up that blonde bombshell he brought to church tonight."

I considered an appropriate comeback, then dismissed the idea. Looking back at Becky, I tried to keep the hurt out of my voice as I said, "See you tomorrow at school—and I'll pick you up Saturday for the canoe trip."

"We'll see," she said evasively. "By the way, Tim, you can paddle with Dennis or someone else, OK?"

"But I thought you and I were going together!"

"Yeah, I know, but I kind of changed my mind." Her voice turned velvety. "You don't mind, do you, Tim?"

Before I could answer, she announced, "I gotta go, OK?"

I sat there like a jerk while she stood up and strutted out the door on the arm of William McAllister the Third. I slumped down in my seat and stared at my melting ice cream. I had a feeling the entire youth group was laughing at me on the sly.

14

I finally convinced Marty to let me tutor him. I went over to his house on Wednesday after school. The place looked cluttered and unattended. Only Marty was there, in Levi's and an unbuttoned shirt, a beer can in one hand, a joint in the other. I followed him into his bedroom.

"Your folks still not around?" I asked as we settled down at his desk.

Marty took a drag on his cigarette. "Naw, they split." I could tell he was trying to sound cool about the whole thing.

I glanced around at his track and field trophies and scholarship citations. They seemed almost lost now amid his rock posters, beer can collection, and smoking paraphernalia. "Your folks are coming back, aren't they? I mean, your mom anyway?"

Marty shrugged. "I got a post card from my old man and his new girl friend in Florida. My ma is off trying to find herself in New York."

"Do the authorities know you're alone?"

"Who knows?"

I picked up a photograph of Marty's junior high football team, wistfully remembering the days when life had some semblance of normalcy for him.

He glanced over at the picture and shook his head. "Can you believe it? The fall of Marty Sullivan!"

I gazed searchingly at him. "What's it like just living here all by yourself?"

Marty flicked his joint into a beanbag ashtray. "Well, it's kind of strange. Kind of feels like you don't belong to anybody. Like nobody really cares."

"I know two people who do."

"Yeah? Who?"

"Me, for one."

"Yeah?" He lifted bleary eyes my way. "And who else?"

"Jesus."

Marty managed a defiant chuckle. "I'd like to see God that way, but I can't. All I can see is the youth group." His lip curled into a sneer. "Did you see the way they stared at Debbie and me in church Sunday night?"

I was silent for a minute, knowing he was dead right. Then I realized something I hadn't considered before. "You can't just look at them, Marty," I said, sitting forward intently. "You gotta look at Jesus. I mean, He didn't hang around with all the straight people. He hung around with sinners. Guys with bad reputations. He ate with them, picked them to be His friends, and called them to righteousness."

"What's this righteousness bit?"

"Right living," I answered.

Marty stared off into space, his eyes expressionless and distant. "I always thought of God as someone standing over me with a big club ready to wail on me if I did anything wrong."

"Well, you can't look at Him like that," I told him.

112

"I mean, God loved us so much that He sent His son to die on a cross for us."

A momentary yearning crossed Marty's face. He remained silent for several minutes, but I could see despair and hope playing against each other in his eyes. Sitting there, sharing his pain, I felt closer to Marty than I had in years.

Finally, he broke the stillness. "I got too many problems in my life right now, Tim. God would just be another complication."

I decided to try another approach. "Our youth group is going on a canoe trip this weekend. I was wondering if you wanted to come?"

He flashed an ironic grin. "Man, you must really think I'm a glutton for punishment, huh?"

"It won't be just guys like Bill and Ron. There are others. And I'll be there, Marty."

"So what am I gonna get from a weekend in the woods with a bunch of guys?"

"Guys? Come on. It's co-ed. You can even bring Debbie along."

"Yeah? Well, let me think about it, okay?"

I had a feeling, by the sudden gleam in Marty's eyes, that he would be there. "We'll take the church bus to the river on Friday night," I told him. "See you in the parking lot at six, okay?"

Sure enough, Marty was there on Friday with his camping gear slung over his shoulder. "Glad you could make it, buddy," I said.

After a long, noisy, bumpy, exhausting ride, we arrived at the riverbank early Saturday morning. The youth group gathered around Steve as he reviewed a map with the route for our canoe trip.

I stepped closer to listen. "Right here is where we

pull in," said Steve. "Just after Three-Mile Bridge. Now do not—I repeat—do not canoe any farther than right here because there's some bad, class-four whitewater, and you don't want to mess with it. Any questions?"

"Can you swim?" Dennis asked Steve.

"Yeah, I can swim. Can you swim?"

Dennis nodded. "Yeah."

"Good. Now, remember, we've got a full day's trip. Don't take it too easy. It'll be getting dark shortly after we get there. And don't worry! The food'll be there when you arrive."

There was a spontaneous cheer when Steve mentioned the chow. He laughed good-naturedly and added, "Make sure you've all got your life preservers on before you get into the canoes, all right?"

I glanced around and spotted Becky standing cozily beside Bill. She was looking up raptly while he discoursed as usual on some weighty subject.

"OK," continued Steve, raising his voice, "everybody have fun, and look out for one another, OK? All right!"

The guys and girls were already dispersing, eager to pull off. As I followed the group toward the riverbank, I noticed Marty standing off by himself, smoking leisurely, looking nonchalant.

As I approached, Bill strode by Marty and warned in his most condescending, Holy Joe voice, "This is a church group. You're not supposed to smoke here!"

With magnificent finesse, Marty inhaled deeply and blew an enormous smoke ring in Bill's face. He coughed and stalked away.

Jennie, Becky's friend, came by too, stopped, looked up at Marty, and gushed, "I'm really glad you could come this weekend."

114

Marty seemed genuinely flattered. He took a drag on his cigarette, then leaned over confidentially. "Thanks, honey. You're kind of cute. Do you want to ride with me?"

Jennie turned on an artificial smile. "Thanks, Marty, but I'm already riding with Jim."

Becky ambled over to Jennie, rolled her eyes at Marty, and said under her breath, "What an idiot!"

I gripped Marty's shoulder and said, "Who you got lined up for your canoe partner, buddy?"

Marty shrugged. "I don't know. Maybe that Jennie babe over there. I figure she's still making up her mind."

"Well, listen, I can go with you in the canoe."

"Naw, you go on. I'll wait a minute longer."

"I'd like to, really."

"See that chick over there?" said Marty, nodding in Traci's direction.

"Yeah. Traci. What about her?"

"She's an OK lady, and she's been eyeing you. You go ride with her."

"You sure, man?"

"Sure, I'm sure."

Everyone ran eagerly to the river's edge and scrambled into their canoes. Ron, Bill, and Becky launched the first one; Dennis, Traci, and I pushed off in the second canoe. A few minutes later, as we bobbed in the calm water, I noticed Marty paddling away from shore alone, without even a life preserver. No one from the other canoes even bothered to look his way.

"Fool," I murmured in frustration. I knew I should have insisted on being his partner no matter what he said.

Our canoes formed a loose-jointed chain as we

115

made our way along the swiftly moving current. Our passage was clear. We roller-coasted over the waves while the blue-green whitecaps eddied and broke over the jutting, jagged rocks.

I got a real rush from the tug and pull of the water as the waves cast their milk-foam froth against our canoe. I could feel the fresh, wet spray tingle in my nostrils and dance on my lips. Every muscle in my body felt alive, invigorated. My senses were heightened by the solidity of the canoe, the grip of the paddle, the moist wind slapping my face and rustling my hair. The river seemed to possess a pulse and will of its own, and we were riding with it, in perfect harmony with its life force.

After awhile, Traci looked around at me from her spot in the middle of the canoe. "Thanks for riding with us, Tim," she murmured, lowering her gaze self-consciously.

"That's OK," I replied and, without thinking, added, "it was Marty's idea."

Becky would have been indignant over such a confession, but Traci just smiled and said, "I like Marty. I've been praying for him, Tim. I know he's going to find Jesus."

"Yeah, I sure hope so," I replied. I glanced back again at Marty—a lone, isolated figure in his canoe. The way our trip was going so far, it looked like the day we were praying for would be a long way off.

When we completed the first leg of our river journey, we all dragged our canoes onto the shore at the designated landing point. Everyone was laughing, wet, sunburned, giddy, and talking at once.

The rest of our counselors were already there in our camping spot, building a fire and preparing the chow.

116

"Hey, we're having hot dogs and hamburgers!" said Dennis. "Can I have both?"

"Why not?" laughed Steve as he set out another stack of beef patties. When he spotted Marty, he flipped a hamburger onto a bun and gave it to him. "The trimmings are over there where Bill and Ron are standing. Help yourself."

When Marty reached the table, Bill and Ron gave him a withering glance. "Hey, I didn't know druggies were invited to this party," Bill said cuttingly.

Ron picked up on the insult. "Better stay out of the water, Marty. Guys who are *stoned* sink right to the bottom."

"Yeah, I know a couple of dudes I'd like to sink," Marty shot back.

Bill and Ron just laughed, pivoted, and smugly ambled away. I could see Marty spit on the ground behind them. I wanted to go after Bill and Ron and put them both in their place, but as I made my way toward them, Dennis stopped me and wanted to socialize. By the time I reached Bill and Ron, they were too absorbed in their own conversation to notice me.

"Angels are non-spacial, supernatural beings able to appear in the temporal, empirical framework—" argued Ron.

"You're talking about an incarnated angelic being, and you know the incarnation happened only once!" intoned Bill loftily.

I spotted Becky hovering idly beside them, looking bored out of her skull. "Aw, come on, you guys," she whined. "I don't even understand what you're talking about!"

Watching Becky, I smiled inwardly with a devious satisfaction. Then I decided I'd better look around for

Marty and smooth things over. When I didn't spot him among the kids around the campfire, I hiked back to the river, asking everyone I passed, "Hey, you seen Marty Sullivan?"

"That hippie? No way," replied Larry.

"Aw, he's probably off tokin' a joint somewhere," laughed another guy.

"Tim, I think he got back in his canoe," said Traci with concern. "He muttered something about going for a ride."

"You're kidding! It's getting dark. Why would he do a fool thing like that?"

"You better tell Steve," she suggested.

"There isn't time!" I ran along the beach to the first canoe I could grab.

"Wait, Tim!" shouted Traci. "Your life jacket— where is it?"

I wasn't about to waste precious seconds worrying about life preservers and recruiting others to look for Marty. Just last week he had considered trying suicide again with that butcher knife on his kitchen table. He hadn't admitted it, and I hadn't confronted him, but we both knew it was true. Now, maybe he was about to make another attempt, this time in a frail canoe in the deadly whitewater Steve had warned us about. In fact, maybe that was why he had insisted on me riding in Traci's canoe.

Even if he wasn't considering suicide, I knew he was depressed over the way the youth group was treating him. That had to be why he had paddled out alone now at nightfall. No doubt he wanted nothing to do with our dismal brand of Christian love.

It was almost dark when I pushed my canoe into the churning current. In the distance I could hear the group singing, "It only takes a spark to get a fire going—" *Man, if only they would put those words into action!*

I paddled my canoe downstream into rough water.

"Soon all those around can warm up to its glowing . . ."

The fading refrains were lost to the deafening roar around me. The river was roiling now, spewing fountains of white, frothing foam. The spumy waves crashed headlong against one another in an incredible, orchestrated dance.

I shouted, "Marty! Marty! Where are you?" But my voice blew back in my face.

About that time, I started praying hard. I was a strong swimmer, but I had no idea how to navigate a whitewater river at night, especially one that was unrunnable. By the pale light of the moon, I maneuvered my canoe among the increasingly treacherous boulders. The rapids, swollen and violent now, tossed my canoe like a toy. I paddled desperately through a twisting, winding gorge, barely riding the surging torrent that flushed downstream with a hypnotizing violence.

I realized then that I was heading for the falls—a deadly twenty-five foot drop. Maybe Marty already went over. He could be dead, for all I knew.

Then another sobering thought struck me: I could die too! Fleetingly, I remembered the Scripture verse I had read in the church sanctuary: *Greater love has no man than to lay down his life for his friends.* The idea of laying down your life for your best friend—it was startling, scary. But it wasn't just a matter of risking my life now for Marty. Everything seemed to be on the line tonight, including giving away all my life to Jesus Christ.

As the river narrowed, the passage grew more harrowing. Tree limbs protruded over the rolling water, and jutting rocks threatened to capsize my canoe.

Then I spotted it! Marty's overturned canoe was perched precariously near the sheer edge of the waterfall, lodged among some rocks, gleaming white in the moonlight.

"Marty!" I shouted frantically. Just then a spiky branch hit my canoe broadside and sent me spinning, taking on water. I grasped the sides of my canoe while a wall of rushing white propelled me toward Marty's upturned craft. "Marty!" I uttered again, choking on a mouthful of bubbly whitewater.

No answer! Had Marty drowned? Been washed over the falls? I shrieked over the roar around me. "Maarty!"

At last I heard his voice, sounding like a thin and distant echo. "Tim!"

"Hold on!" I shouted. I pushed my canoe into an eddy among several boulders, groped under the seat for the rope and, fighting the waves, tied it to an overhanging branch. I maneuvered through the frenzied rapids toward Marty's canoe. I could see him now—mere feet from the treacherous falls, in a pocket of churning water, gripping the canoe's gunwales, gasping for breath.

"Ca-can't hold on," he rasped.

I tossed him the rope, but he missed it. His hands slipped from the canoe. "God—Tim!" he cried. "I don't want to die!"

Like a madman, I vaulted from my canoe onto the sleek, slippery hulk of his overturned craft, clutched Marty's arm, and struggled to haul him onto his canoe. He had the rope now. "Tim, buddy," he coughed. He was getting his second wind, dragging himself toward the safety of the rocks.

Then, without warning, a billowing wave heaved against me, catapulting me into a dizzying whirlpool. I felt myself thrust by the bone-chilling current toward the precipice. Suddenly, I was plummeting, shooting down the gushing rapids like a wet eel sliding down a jet stream. Flailing my arms and gulping water, I sank into a dark, icy, spinning sea of oblivion.

15

10:10 p.m. Leech Lake General Hospital Emergency Room:

"Concussion . . . multiple fractures . . . loss of blood," a doctor was saying.

"Doctor, his blood pressure is dropping," cried a nurse.

"Pulse?"

"Erratic."

"Check his pupils. Where's the X-ray?"

"His pupils are dilated,"said the nurse.

"Call for an X-ray!"

"X-ray, stat!"

"There's no pulse, doctor!" said the nurse in alarm. "Pressure's bottomed out!"

"The defibrilator!" ordered the doctor. "Quick, the paddles, over here! Stand clear!"

"Still no pulse, doctor!"

The physician positioned the paddles a second time.

"Come on, again! Do it! Here, again! Come on, kiddo! You can't die!"

"It's no use, doctor. He's gone."

"I won't let him go! He's just a kid—just a kid! Here,

again, the paddles! One more time!"

10:15 p.m. North of Chicago, heading toward Leech Lake:

An automobile raced north through the Chicago suburbs, careening through the darkened, rain-drenched streets. Sid Hughes sat behind the wheel, tense with alarm, straining to see past the noisy, swishing windshield wipers through the wet, murky haze ahead. Meg sat beside him, stunned, shivering, hugging her arms against her chest as if to ward off invisible terrors of the night.

"With this awful weather," she murmured, "the drive will take forever. The hospital didn't say how bad Tim was—how serious?"

"It's serious, Meg."

"How do you know?"

"An emergency flight—by helicopter? I know it's serious."

"Would you pray with me, Sid?" Meg asked softly.

"Pray? Meg, this isn't the time for that," Sid barked.

"If this isn't the time, Sid, then when is?"

After a moment of silence, Meg cried, "You still haven't given me a straight answer, Sid. Would you please pray with me?"

"Yeah, yeah," he snapped. "Do what you want."

"Dear Lord," she began, then hesitated.

"Well, come on!" growled Sid. "You got the guy's attention already! Say something!"

"Dear Lord," Meg said again, faltering, "we need You right now, so much. We've never admitted it before, but we need You to help Timmy—Oh, God, we don't want to lose our son. Please, God, let him live!"

10:18 p.m. Emergency Waiting Room, Leech Lake General:

A group of frightened, ragtag teenagers lingered in the stark, sterile waiting room, hovering together aimlessly, silent, subdued. Their eyes were wide with disbelief, their throats knotted with a tight, unspoken pain. Their stomachs churned with apprehension and revolted against the heavy, antiseptic hospital smells. Steve, their leader, moved among them, gripping shoulders in encouragement, whispering words of comfort. "Hey, kids, let's form a circle and join hands," he suggested, "and pray right here and now for Tim!"

As they prayed, visitors and patients, doctors and nurses paused and looked on, hushed and marveling.

10:22 p.m. Leech Lake General Emergency Room:

A nurse exclaimed excitedly, "I've got a pulse, doctor!"

"Blood pressure's coming back up!"

"Thank God!"declared the doctor. "This boy's going to make it after all. It's a miracle!"

Three days later. Intensive Care Unit:

Consciousness. It was returning in faint, fleeting glimmers. But mostly there were shadows. I was surrounded by a pervasive darkness, aware only of a pressure in my head, binding, oppressive. I tried to speak, but I couldn't shake off the drugged sleep that immobilized me. I was aware of voices sounding muffled and distant. Then I realized it was Mom and Dad talking quietly. When I tried to move, my entire body ached. Was I paralyzed? Dying?

"How is he, nurse?" I heard Mom ask.

"He's holding his own."

"But he's still in a coma!"

"I know. But at least he's off the respirator and breathing on his own. Now we just have to wait. We have to give it time."

"It's been three days already," complained Dad, sounding more frightened than angry. "We still don't know whether or not Tim has suffered any—brain damage."

I tried to move my lips, but they were cracked and dry. My tongue felt thick and numb. I wanted desperately to reach out and comfort my parents, but I couldn't even lift my eyelids. "Please, Lord," I begged silently, "Mom and Dad still need me. Just give me one more chance. One more chance to stand up for You!"

With all the effort I could summon I forced open my eyes and blinked against the brightness of my hospital room. I uttered one word: "Mom!"

Then I felt both my parents leaning over me, touching my face, weeping. "Get the doctor, Sid." cried Mom. "Get the doctor! Our son's waking up at last!"

Gradually, after coming out of the coma, I learned what a miracle it was that I had survived. Amazingly, Jesus had answered my prayer before I was even conscious enough to form the words. And He had answered my mother's prayer and the earnest prayers of my friends. I felt awed and grateful beyond words that God had given me a second chance at life.

Slowly, I began to put the pieces of my life and memory together again. For several days I had the worst headache I'd ever had in my seventeen years! I had to stay in the hospital for three weeks, my head bandaged like a mummy's, my leg in a cast, but Mom and Dad were at my bedside every chance they got.

Every time Mom saw me, she murmured, "Thank God you're alive, Timmy!" Dad always gave her his perturbed glance and muttered, "Cut the mush, Meg," but he said it with tears in his eyes.

As soon as I was out of intensive care, my friends came to visit. Marty came every day. We were closer than we'd ever been. I'd saved his life, but he'd turned right around and saved mine—struggling over the rocky ledge along the river, scrambling to the bottom of the falls and fishing me out of the water. But then, maybe neither of us would have made it if Traci hadn't sent Steve and the other guys out looking for us.

Anyway, Marty and I didn't talk much about it. We laughed and made jokes about the cute nurses and the lousy hospital food. We reminisced about the pranks we played as kids and the carefree summers we spent fishing and hiking.

I learned from Traci that Marty had started coming to the Bible club at school. "Would you believe, he brought his whole gang with him! He's telling everyone that the Lord saved his life." She smiled shyly. "He's back in his classes too, Tim. I'm helping him catch up. He really wants to turn his life around."

It was six weeks before I was able to return to school—and then I had to walk on crutches. But I didn't mind. I was just glad to be alive.

And I was excited about what was happening at Roosevelt High. Jesus was becoming real to a lot of the kids. In the next few weeks, our Bible study tripled in size. Becky and her friends started attending and taking an active part. But best of all, Marty had asked the Lord into his life, and he didn't care who knew it!

I'm not saying everything was perfect after that, but

for the first time in my life I felt like I knew who I was and where I was going. I didn't have to walk in my dad's shadow or in Marty's shadow any longer. I could be myself—the person Jesus wanted me to be.

Sure, my dad still didn't understand it all, but he tried to be a little more tolerant. And Mom—well, I had a feeling she was ready to hear about Jesus, and I was beginning to find a few words here and there to tell her. I'd begged God for one more chance to tell others about Him. Now, one by one, He was giving me opportunities to share His love.

But I sensed that the Lord still had something more in mind for me. Then, about three weeks after I'd returned to school, the principal called a special assembly. Even my parents were invited to attend. When I learned that I was to be the guest of honor, I knew this was the ultimate test. Could I speak out for Jesus in an auditorium filled with high school kids—and my parents?

The assembly began with a lofty speech from the principal. "Since Roosevelt was founded forty years ago," he intoned dramatically, "only four students have been honored to receive the prestigious Francis J. Corboy Award for notable acts of selfless devotion to their fellow man. Today, it is my privilege to honor yet a fifth recipient of this coveted award. I now call upon the vice-president of the junior class, Martin M. Sullivan, to present the award."

Enthusiastic applause erupted from the audience as Marty strolled over to the podium and took the microphone. "Thank you, thank you, but please save your big guns for the next guy!"

Marty waited for everyone to settle down. Then he said earnestly, "A couple of months ago I went on a church camping trip in Minnesota. I went out in this canoe by myself because I kinda felt rejected by the group. It got dark, but I kept going because I felt so bad inside. Then I got caught in some bad whitewater, and I thought I was gonna drown."

Marty's voice wavered with emotion. "I couldn't believe what happened next. I saw Tim coming to help me, and I thought, What's this crazy guy doing fighting the rapids, looking for a burnout like me?" Marty blinked rapidly. "I'll tell ya, man! It was just like the Lord, because Tim got all messed up trying to save my life." He stopped, too choked up to continue. There was dead silence in the auditorium.

Finally, Marty coughed and regained his composure. He picked up a shiny plaque from the podium. "So anyway, the school has decided to give this award to Tim Hughes, my best friend!"

Everyone clapped loudly. I looked over at Mom and Dad. They were smiling with a tenderness and pride I'd never seen before. Mom's face looked young and smooth again, free of tension for the first time in weeks. Several guys nudged me and said, "Go on up, Tim."

My dad leaned over and warned, "Just don't start talking about religion, Tim."

"Oh, Sid," chided Mom. "He wouldn't do that in front of all these people!"

I just smiled and made my way to the front, still limping a little, then waited until it was quiet. My heart was pounding like a drum. I figured the sound must be echoing through the whole auditorium. I sent up a fast prayer for calm and courage.

"Instead of talking about myself or some heroic deed that any of you would have done if you had been in my shoes, I'd like to give some credit to a real hero." I stopped and took a deep breath. "A little while ago, I probably could have talked to you about a famous athlete or musician, but I wouldn't have been able to talk to you about my real hero. I was too ashamed."

I waited while a murmur rose from the audience.

Raising my voice a notch, I said fervently, "Now I realize that my hero was never ashamed. He was born in an eating trough for animals and He died on a garbage mound between two criminals. He ate with prostitutes and thieves. He washed his friends' feet and submitted himself to public mockery without saying a word."

Amazingly, everyone was listening raptly. I even spotted Dad dabbing his eyes with Mom's handkerchief.

"But He didn't die because He had to," I declared with conviction. "He died for you and me because He loves us. His name is Jesus Christ. And He's alive today. He's right here in this assembly, and He wants to come into your hearts and be part of your lives. I hope you let Him come in. Thank you."

There was a long moment of silence, followed by a ripple of applause. Then, before I knew it, everyone was standing and clapping thunderously. Dad was beaming; Mom was weeping. Marty came over and swung his arm around my shoulder and raised his hand in a victory sign. We gave each other an old bear hug right there on stage while everyone in Roosevelt High Auditorium whistled and hooted and clapped.

Talk about rare moments you stamp in your memory for all time! Standing up for Jesus beside my best friend was the most incredible experience of my life. And I'm not ashamed to admit it!